A LESSON IN MURDER

A DI Kate Medlar novel

Lin Bird

Tim Saunders Publications

TS

Copyright © 2023 Lin Bird

All rights reserved

The characters and events portrayed in this book are fictitious. Any similarity to real persons, living or dead, is coincidental and not intended by the author.

No part of this book may be reproduced, or stored in a retrieval system, or transmitted in any form or by any means, electronic, mechanical, photocopying, recording, or otherwise, without express written permission of the publisher.

Cover design: John Atkinson
www.johnatkinson-artist.com

For Katie and Gemma

Hope you like Kate!

Lui Bird

MEDLAR

PROLOGUE

Transcript Audio Log 2mins 34secs

An hour after Izzy had taken in the supper tray I stood outside the door of her sitting room. I knocked. There was no reply. That was promising. I knocked again, to be sure. Nothing. I tugged on a glove, turned the handle and walked in. The room was gloomy with just the one lamp on the desk as the only source of light. She was still at her desk but the remains on the supper tray indicated she had eaten the snack that I had so carefully prepared. I walked forward, pulling on the second glove. It looked as if she had fallen asleep. She had slumped back in her high backed chair and her head had slipped to one side. A pool of drool had collected on the left shoulder of her dress. Not so elegant now!

    I tapped her on the hand. No response. I tapped a little harder. Nothing. I even had the temerity to slap her on the face, but not hard. She was out cold. It had worked. I reached into my bag and pulled out two silk scarves and folded them into broad bands and used them to tie her wrists to her chair arms. I'd heard somewhere that silk doesn't leave marks. I hoped this was right. Then I pulled out the plastic wrap. The gloves were a hindrance and in the end I slipped them off and began to wind the film wrap around her head, paying particular attention to covering her mouth and nose. Even before I'd finished she'd began to make snuffling sounds and deep inarticulate moans. I didn't need to hear this so I picked up the supper tray and swiftly left the room.

The corridors were quieter now but the tray gave me permission to still be roaming. Back in the staff kitchen I washed and tidied away the crockery from the tray. I swept the crumbs into the food waste and the plastic wrap I wiped and threw into the recycling bag. Satisfied that was all as it should be I returned to the sitting room.

Again I knocked. Partly habit, partly for the benefit of anyone who might pass by, although there was no-one in sight. It would be lights out in about half-an-hour. She was where I'd left her. I felt for a pulse. The skin was still warm and, at first, I thought that I'd failed but there was no pulse. There was no gently rising and falling movement in her chest.

Carefully, I unwound the plastic wrap, ensuring that every piece came away. I fluffed up her hair a little at the sides where they had been flattened. I unwound the silk scarves and checked for marks on her wrists, but they were clear. I stepped back to look at the scene with fresh eyes. It looked as if she had fallen asleep. There was nothing more for me to do, so I left. She would be found at some point and they would think she'd died of a heart attack or a stroke. No-one would know she has been punished for her wickedness.

Back in the staff room kitchen I threw the remains of the plastic wrap into the recycling and took it and the food waste bag out to the main bins. It was collection day the following day. If anyone thought to find evidence it would be long gone.

CHAPTER 1

Kate Medlar, Detective Inspector Kate Medlar stood looking at the two slices of bread on her kitchen counter and wondering whether additional penicillin was good for you. Her red gold hair, not ginger, she insisted, glowed in the early morning light. She wore it short because if it grew longer it also grew wider! The pixie haircut and her slight frame gave her an inappropriately fragile look, which many criminals had lived to rue.

She sighed deeply. She really must get herself into a routine that allowed for shopping. She had only been in Eashire seven weeks. Had found out on day one that you made it sound like Escher, "Like the artist," her Detective Constable, Colm Hunter had said, and that life in a shire town was very different from the city.

Suddenly the air was alive with the chorus from Blondie's song 'Don't leave me hanging on the telephone'. It was her mobile's ring tone. Kate saw it was her boss, Detective Chief Inspector Bartholomew. Bart behind his back but never to his face. Kate's heart lifted. If Bart was calling her outside office hours then something had happened.

"Morning sir."

"Morning Kate. I have a suspicious death for you."

"Yes, sir."

"Headmistress of Blaiseforth Manor."

Kate wrinkled her forehead in confusion. "I thought she died of a heart attack, a couple of days ago." Then her brow cleared as she realised what must have happened, and she added, "What did the post-mortem throw up?"

"She was found in her sitting room three mornings ago. Everyone thought it was a heart attack. Even Gus!" Gus Lipstein, the town's leading pathologist. Well, in fairness their only pathologist and then they had to share him with the rest of the county.

"So what made Gus change his mind? I assume he called you first thing?"

"The toxicology came back this morning. Her blood was swamped with a tranquiliser. Gus said that alone might have eventually led to her death but with getting those results he took another look at the body and found other inconsistencies. He'd like you to go over as soon as possible."

"Yes sir."

"What are you and Colm working on at the moment?"

"Just that fracas in the Bull & Frog on Saturday."

"Pass what you've got and what you were planning to do next to DS Coles, Jan can follow up on whatever you've got."

"Yes sir. Shall I take DC Hunter with me?"

"Yes. He knows the area. You can have Sergeant Hughes to run your murder book and boards. I'll rustle up a couple of uniforms for you to do the grunt work."

"Thank you sir. What about a forensic team?"

"I'll put them on stand-by but I'd like you to break the news personally before the dust brigade turn up."

"Right, sir. I'll ring you when we've spoken to Gus and we'll synchronise forensics then."

"I'll wait for your call."

Kate thought he was about to hang up but instead he said, "Tread carefully with this one Kate. The great and good of Eashire do not like their lives touched by crime. Any kind of crime."

"Yes sir."

This time he did put the phone down.

Kate quickly called DS Coles and gave her the details she would need to follow up on the Bull & Frog dispute and then she called Colm Hunter.

"Morning Colm. Can you meet me at the morgue by nine? We have a suspicious death."

There was a note of excitement in Colm's voice, "Sure, boss. I'm on the other side of town at the moment so I'll meet you there."

"Ok. Outside the mortuary at nine." She shut off the phone and returned to the bread. It wouldn't taste too bad as toast she reassured herself. She certainly wasn't going to visit the mortuary on an empty stomach.

CHAPTER 2

Kate spotted Colm leaning against one of the pillars that framed the entrance to the mortuary. He wore his dark hair short but the buffeting wind had still managed to find enough to play with. As Kate slipped into what seemed to be the last parking space, she reflected that Colm was a good looking man in that homely, comforting sort of way, more the build of a farmer, she thought. His saving grace was his smile that changed a placid unremarkable face into an intelligent observer.

Stepping towards him he spotted her and moved his broad shoulders to push himself upright. "Morning boss."

"Okay Colm. Let's go see what Gus has to say."

Stepping into the quiet of the foyer they were greeted by the receptionist, who recognised Colm, "Morning, the professor is expecting you. Theatre three." She waved towards the first of the double doors.

As they stepped into the neon lit corridor Colm muttered, "Oh wow!" The smells of disinfectant and decomposition vied for dominance and it seemed the decomp was winning. The smell was so strong Kate was sure she could taste it.

They pushed hurriedly into theatre three

where Professor Gus Lipstein awaited them with a sheeted body in front of him.

"Wow, prof, that's some stink out there!" Colm said, trying to blow the smell out of his nostrils.

Although his face said stern, Gus' eyes twinkled, "It's not often my theatre is chosen in preference to the surrounds!" Checking a clipboard on the trolley he continued. "We had two homeless people brought in this morning. They were found under the Marston Bridge. I'm thinking they've been there for a couple of weeks, maybe more."

"Poor sods," Colm said with feeling.

"Now, Detective Inspector Medlar, our suspicious death." He looked down at the covered corpse before consulting his clipboard again. "Elise Betteridge, aged sixty-two, found dead three mornings ago. Assumed heart attack." He lay the clipboard down and turned back the sheet to reveal a trim looking woman; a good looking woman if you ignored the 'y' incision and the obvious cuts around the head.

Kate bent forward, "She looks good for her age."

"I agree. Which is why when her heart appeared to be in fine order I began to consider more sinister causes, hence the rush I put on the toxicology and stomach contents analysis. I also checked her cranium, both externally and internally, and all was fine there as well." Gus went back to perusing his notes.

"So tranquilisers?" Kate asked. "Deliberate overdose?"

Gus shook his head. "Unlikely. The tranquiliser was ketamine and she had enough in her system to fell an elephant."

"Ketamine?" Colm asked.

Gus nodded and added, "Surprisingly not as much of a problem in Eashire as you would think, given our rural predominance."

Kate said, "I can't see a headmistress of a prestigious girls' school having access to street drugs."

"Unlikely," Gus confirmed.

"What form does ketamine take?" Colm asked.

"You can get it in liquid form, but that tends to be medicinal grade. Street versions tend to be powder. Sometimes cut with other substances," Gus informed them.

"Wouldn't she taste it if it was added to food?" Kate asked.

"It is very bitter apparently, but I suppose it would depend what it was put in."

"So stomach contents?"

Gus checked his board again, "Close to death she consumed fruit cake and hot chocolate. I think both were laced with the ketamine. Earlier she had a more substantial meal but I am sure the ketamine was in the cake and drink."

"So whoever did it wasn't leaving anything to

chance, were they?"

"No the dose was enormous."

"So death by poisoning?" Kate summarised.

"Well, I'm not sure," Gus said. He beckoned for them to come closer. "Once I was thinking suspicious death I went over Miss Betteridge again and found the following," he pointed to her eyes. "There is evidence of petechial haemorrhage in the eyes and inside area of the lips." Gus produced a magnifying glass and altered the overhead light for Kate and Colm to see.

"And you'll also notice a blue tinge around her lips and nose. In the first instance I thought they were not inconsistent with heart failure."

Kate tried to keep her breathing shallow as she peered closely at the dead woman's eyes and mouth.

"And," Gus said with a flourish, "what do you make of these?" He pulled out both arms and pointed to almost invisible marks on the woman's wrists.

Kate looked closer. If Gus hadn't pointed them out she wouldn't have noticed the slight blueish tinge to areas around the wrist. "She was tied down?" she asked.

"I think that may be a possible cause. But your perpetrator obviously did not use cord or rope. They would have left very distinctive marks."

"So, it seems we have overkill," Kate said,

running through the scenario in her head. "She was knocked out with ketamine, tied down and then suffocated? Anything in her mouth or nose to indicate what she was suffocated with?"

Gus shook his head. "Can you establish that at all" Kate asked hopefully. "What about time of death?"

"From the state of the stomach contents I would say she died within two hours of having had her hot chocolate and fruit cake. Find out when she had those and you have a reasonably good time of death."

"I suppose we'd better go and try and establish a crime scene, then," said Colm.

"Yes we must. Thanks Professor."

"My pleasure, DI Medlar."

CHAPTER 3

On the way back to her car Kate phoned DCI Bartholomew and brought him up to date. "So it looks like our killer was leaving nothing to chance. I think he or she were thinking a death with no outward signs would be accepted without a post-mortem."

"I'm assuming you are off to Blaiseforth Manor now?" Bart asked.

"Yes sir. If you could ask forensics to turn up," she checked her watch, nine-forty.

She mouthed to Colm, "How long to get to the school?"

Colm held out both hands and flashed his fingers twice.

Kate double checked and mouthed "Twenty?"

Colm nodded.

"At eleven. That will give me chance to talk to whoever is acting as Head and sound out the situation."

"Okay, Kate. Hughes has set your incident up in room eleven."

Kate had no idea where room eleven was but said, "Thank you, sir."

Once she'd hung up Kate asked, "Room eleven?"

Colm groaned, "It's a good size room but it's

right at the top of the building, in the eaves. It's really hot up there."

Since Kate was shivering with the cold as she got into her car the thought of a hot room was far from unpleasant. Kate was sat in the passenger seat of her own car, "You drive, Colm, you know where you're going and I can have a look at the school website."

Blaiseforth Manor was five or six miles north of Eashire. As Colm drove, Kate did a quick internet search. Blaiseforth alumni featured a plethora of famous and noble names in the county. In addition their local MP was an ex-Blaiseforth pupil, as was the Chief Constable. Mentally Kate reminded herself of Bart's words, 'tread gently' in her dealings with the school.

The school had been a bequest of one Gladstone Blaiseforth in the early 1900s. For a man of his time he was very far thinking. He had been disappointed that his daughter had limited access to mainstream education because of her sex. He recognised her talents and undertook to teach her himself. A well respected lawyer with decades of experience he had given it all to Georgina Blaiseforth, who in turn had dominated the legal system of Eashire until the beginning of the Second World War. However, Gladstone was not completely forward thinking. At his death Georgina's cousin, Edward Blaiseforth became owner of the Blaiseforth estate but not the Manor, that was to become a school for girls 'of local, respectable Eashire families', funded by a trust he set up. Today the local element was not the only criteria. In fact, Kate thought, looking at the school fees, the only real criteria was the ability to pay.

Kate looked up from her small screen. Terraced houses gave way to semis and detached, with their bits of garden, which in turn gave way to hedgerows and open fields. Kate still wondered at the colours of the fields and trees once outside the town centre. She'd lived all her life in cities and rarely took advantage of the parks they possessed. Now she was surrounded by nature. Even in this dead season of winter she noticed that some small trees had red stems and that the white bark of one type of tree stuck out like bones. That the soil had a reddish hue under the silver glint of the unyielding frost.

A copse of trees indicated the start of the school's land and soon Colm was turning onto the drive, steering between two brick built columns capped with a pair of birds. Kate couldn't make out the species but not eagles, she was sure. The sign at the side indicated that the school took both boarders and day girls. Kate supposed that there were enough wealthy families in the shire to provide a good source of day girls.

The drive ended in front of the Georgian façade, 'The most delectable example of Georgian architecture, untouched in over 250 years', Kate had read the school prospectus online. "Imagine coming to this every day," Colm said with genuine awe.

Kate was non-committal in her "Umm!" What she did note was that there were security cameras at the gates and on the building. She made a mental note to get those checked.

They made their way up a shallow staircase to impressive double doors, which opened onto a foyer. To one side Kate spotted a door with Reception picked out in gold lettering. She knocked and walked in. An elderly woman, greying hair shoved haphazardly into a bun, gave them a startled look through thick glass lenses.

Kate pulled out her identity card and held it out, "Detective Inspector Kate Medlar and my colleague, Detective Constable Hunt," Kate nodded her head towards Colm.

"We wish to talk to the deputy headteacher, please," Kate glanced at the wooden name block on the table, "Mrs Jessop."

The introductions seemed to increase Mrs Jessop's unease. "Oh my. Really. It's not a good time, you know. I don't know if Miss Sandford.." she trailed off.

"I quite understand, but this is a police matter and we will need to talk to Miss Sandford."

Mrs Jessop stood up. It was the first time that Kate had actually seen the action of wringing one's hands. "Yes, of course. If I could ask you to wait in the hall I will go and fetch Miss Sandford."

Colm and Kate preceded Mrs Jessop into the hall. As Mrs Jessop scuttled off, her quick tapping feet echoing in the corridor, Kate stood looking at the Honours board displaying a list of head girls since the Manor's inception as a school in 1904. She noted that both an E Betteridge and an E Sandford had been head girls in the early 1970s.

CHAPTER 4

Within a few minutes they could hear again the hastening footsteps of Mrs Jessop and firmer, steadier steps accompanying them. Miss Sandford was a tall woman, at least six foot, Kate thought, feeling her own lack of stature. She wore a good quality but plain linen sage green dress, with a cream belt its only adornment. Her greying hair was cut into a long bob and shone with good health. She came towards Kate and held her hand out, "Officers. I believe you need to speak with me?"

Once again they showed their identity cards and made their introductions.

"Medlar. As in the fruit? How very unusual." Miss Sandford smiled as she led them into her office. Kate smiled in response. It wasn't often people knew about the Medlar fruit. The office was large. Kate thought her entire cottage would fit within its walls. To one side were a conference table and chairs and to the other, comfortable easy chairs. Ahead was the desk.

Miss Sandford pointed them towards two chairs one side of the desk and took the office chair behind, for herself. "Now, what can I do for you? I am sure you are aware that the school has recently lost its headteacher and I am acting Head for the time being, but obviously I will help you in any way I can."

Kate gauged the woman opposite her. She was calm and attentive. No sign that anything was being hidden. Some tension but that was to be expected, given the circumstances. "It's about Miss Betteridge's death that we are here," Kate began.

Miss Sandford's eyebrows rose enquiringly. "It was a heart attack! Wasn't it?"

"At this stage we are not sure but the autopsy has revealed a number of complications that we need to clarify."

Miss Sandford rocked back in her chair and blew out her lips. "What sort of complications? Are you saying she didn't die of natural causes?" Her voice rose in disbelief.

"We are treating it as suspicious at the moment. As I said. There are some elements that we need to explain."

Miss Sandford rocked back to the desk and placed her forearms on the surface. Leaning forward she said in a clear, firm voice, "Anything I, or the school can do to help with your investigation, we will do."

"Thank you. Can I just ask you to go over events of the morning Miss Betteridge was found?"

Miss Sandford nodded.

"So who found Miss Betteridge?"

"It was me. I.." She tailed off. Collecting her thoughts. "Normally Elise and I would meet, at about eight, to compare diaries and discuss things for the day ahead. When she didn't turn up I was.." Again she halted. "I don't know, uneasy? It was so unlike Elise to be late for anything." She gave a subdued laugh, "She was one of those people who would rather be an hour early than a minute late."

Kate nodded encouragingly and Miss Sandford returned to her narrative. "I know she often gets up early to finish paperwork, so I wondered whether she had lost track of time. I went to her sitting room and knocked. There was no reply but when I tried the handle it was not locked. Elise always keeps it locked if she is elsewhere." Again she came to a halt and her hand trembled slightly as she tucked one side of her hair behind her ear. "I knocked again and then went in. She looked asleep. She was still wearing the clothes from the day before and I thought she had been working all night and fallen asleep." She was agitated. This was clearly painful.

Kate leant forward and touched her gently on the arm. "Did the sitting room look as it always did? Nothing out of place?"

Miss Sandford hesitated and Kate was aware that she had gone inside herself and revisited the room. Slowly she shook her head, "No, it was as it always is."

"So Miss Betteridge looked as if she were asleep?"

Miss Sandford took a deep breath and nodded. "I called her name as I walked across the room and touched her lightly on the hand. I didn't want to scare her to death!" She gasped and put her hand to her mouth, realising what she had said.

Kate made a calming motion with her hand and Miss Sandford continued. "Her hand was icy cold and she didn't respond. I jiggled her shoulder but it was clear she was dead. I think I may have blacked out for a few minutes with shock. When I was aware again my heart was hammering and I was reaching for the telephone and dialling 999." She leant back in her chair again as if spent.

"Thank you, Miss Sandford, I know that was not easy."

Miss Sandford closed her eyes and nodded.

"So I assume that when the ambulance arrived they pronounced her dead and surmised she'd had a heart attack as there were no other signs?"

Miss Sandford nodded again.

"Could I suggest that we ask Mrs Jessop for some tea before we continue?" Colm proposed.

CHAPTER 5

"First impressions?" Kate asked.

"She was genuinely upset about finding the body," said Colm. "And did you notice how she hopped from past to present tense. She hasn't got it clear in her head yet."

Kate looked thoughtful. "It wouldn't be the first time a murderer has baulked at seeing their crime completed. But, no, at the moment, I agree."

The entrance of the tea tray was heralded by the clatter of china and the tinkle of spoons. Miss Sandford opened the door and Mrs Jessop followed with the tray. "Put it on the conference table, Barbara." Miss Sandford pointed to the side, "Thank you." As Mrs Jessop placed it carefully on the wood and scurried out.

Time was taken up making tea and selecting biscuits. Once they were sat again, Kate having checked her watch, continued. "In about thirty minutes our forensic team will be here. They will need to investigate the room where Miss Betteridge was found dead."

"Oh, I.." Miss Sandford faltered. "I think the domestic staff will have cleaned Miss Betteridge's sitting room since then."

Kate's heart sank. "Did a police officer not attend when you dialled 999?"

"Oh yes, but everyone was happy that it was a heart attack... I suppose he thought it was an ordinary death."

Inwardly Kate cursed. What blithering idiot hadn't had the presence of mind not to seal the room until the autopsy results were in? Of course they would have cleaned the room. She rallied. "We'll let forensics decide what they may be able to do. I would also like them to have access to your CCTV footage. I'm assuming your cameras record?"

Miss Sandford appeared troubled, whether in regret for the domestic staff's actions or that a forensic team would be in the school. And then said, "Of course, you can have the footage. Ask Barbara for the access code."

Kate got back to her questions. "Can you talk me through Miss Betteridge's last day?"

Miss Sandford looked uneasy.

"You say you normally met to discuss the day?" Kate prompted.

Miss Sandford pushed her cup and saucer to one side and nodded in agreement.

"Had anything out of the ordinary happened in the days before her death?" Kate asked.

Miss Sandford reached for the large desk diary and then used the computer mouse to pull up something on the screen. Having checked, she began. "Unexpectedly, Elise had a meeting on Monday with an architectural team and some other group," she paused and looked directly at

Kate, "At that point I did not know who this other group were or why they attended the meeting."

Colm asked, "But you knew about the architects?"

Miss Sandford smiled, "We were fortunate enough to be left a legacy by a past pupil and that, in addition to the fundraising we have been doing for the last year, has given us enough to think about rebuilding a more modern media and theatre studio."

"So this unknown group could have been specialists in that field?" Kate asked.

Miss Sandford nodded, "So I assumed at the time." She looked back at the screen. "This unexpected meeting was to last most of the day. The results of that meeting were then conveyed to some of the staff and trustees in a special meeting," Kate heard the emphasis in Miss Sandford's tone. "That evening. Apparently Elise had emailed the trustees over the weekend." Now Kate heard a bitter edge.

"Did this change in her activities for the day create any problems?"

Miss Sandford closed her eyes briefly, "No, not really. Elise did very little teaching and one of the department heads did her lunchtime duty, so no. No real impact."

"I'm assuming your special meeting was to reveal the conclusions from the architects and the other group?" Kate queried.

Miss Sandford nodded. "Yes. It became

apparent that the unknown group were actually representatives from an American college who wanted to establish a base in Britain, specifically for the families of Americans deployed here." Miss Sandford's voice was flat.

Kate was unable to decide whether Miss Sandford was for or against this plan. She probed, "So how was that received by the departments and trustees?"

"Very mixed. Some were immediately for it and others were not as sure." Whether she was going to give her own opinion they were not to know for at that moment a bell sounded and the call of girls' voices echoed through to them. Miss Sandford started and checked her watch. "I'm sorry, could we continue this at a later time? I'm due to teach Year 9, science," she grimaced. Kate was unsure whether it was Year 9 or the science that caused the wince.

"Of course. Could you ask Mrs Jessop to allocate us a room so we can carry out interviews without inconveniencing you?" Kate asked.

Miss Sandford was already on the move. "Yes. Ask her to set up the meeting room for you."

CHAPTER 6

As Miss Sandford's footsteps retreated, Kate knocked on the reception door again and strode in. Mrs Jessop seemed as startled by their presence now as she had the first time. Having explained Miss Sandford's instructions Mrs Jessop led them to the meeting room. It was large, set up like conferences Kate had attended in hotels; a podium area and tables scattered around the room with seating.

"I can get you some water and glasses, if you wish?" Miss Jessop asked.

"That would be lovely," Colm smiled and Mrs Jessop blushed.

"Before you do that could we ask you a few questions first?" asked Kate pointing to the closest table and chairs.

"I really can't leave the office," Mrs Jessop's voice quavered.

"No problem, we'll come to you then," said Colm leading Mrs Jessop out with a wave of his arm.

Back in the reception office Kate and Colm pulled two chairs up to Mrs Jessop's desk. Kate began, "You must hear a lot of what goes on in the school in here."

Mrs Jessop bridled. "I am not a gossip!"

Colm calmly intervened, "We believe that

someone as experienced as yourself must become a confidante of many of the staff and pupils. And I expect Miss Betteridge would have been lost without you."

Mrs Jessop visibly relaxed and she smiled wanly. "Well, yes. I have been receptionist and secretary here for almost twenty-five years."

Kate tried to look suitably impressed. "Thank goodness Miss Sandford has your support at this trying time."

Colm nodded in agreement. "Now we understand that on Monday, Miss Betteridge had an unexpected meeting with several people? Were you involved in that?"

Mrs Jessop looked a little affronted and gave the impression of a dismissive sniff, "Well, I brought them tea and coffee and organised their lunch. Of course the bulk of the work was in the evening, getting the paperwork ready for the special meeting. I was at the photocopier for hours."

Whatever else she was going to say was interrupted by a sharp knock at the door. Kate vaguely recognised the bushy eyebrowed face that peered round the edge of the door, "Ah, DI Medlar. Mike Edwards. My team and I are at your disposal."

Kate turned back to Mrs Jessop, "My apologies Mrs Jessop but would you please take us to Miss Betteridge's room?"

Now Mrs Jessop really was flustered. "Miss

Betteridge's room? I, er..."

Colm stepped in with his reassuring smile and calm, "It's all right. Miss Sandford knows that our team were coming in."

That seemed to calm her and she began to rummage in a drawer in her desk. Finally she held up, triumphantly, a key, "Her room will be locked, so you will need this." She then led everyone out of the room. She paused again when she saw the extent of Mike Edwards' team. "This way."

Mrs Jessop led them up the central staircase onto the first landing. Miss Betteridge's room was directly ahead. She went forward to place the key in the lock but Edwards interrupted her movement. "Thank you, we'll take over from here."

He crouched down and examined the round brass door knob. Extracting a pencil torch from his breast pocket, he rose. "No prints. It's been polished clean."

He unlocked the door and turned the handle, stepping back to allow Kate and Colm to precede him into the room, having checked that they now wore forensic gloves and booties. Kate strode in and was temporarily blinded by the winter sun pouring through a large bay window, which housed an old fashioned desk. The air smelt of polish and potpourri.

To the right two comfortable fireside chairs had their backs to the room, hunched around the fire and a tall coffee table stood between them. Kate could see in her mind's eye the supper tray being placed there and Miss Betteridge retiring to the more comfortable chair whilst she had her supper. To the left of the room was a display cabinet with various glass and china knick-knackery on display. In the left hand corner, before the bay started was another fireside type chair. A large office chair was tucked under the desk.

Edwards' team flowed in around them. He turned to Kate, "Where was the body found?"

Kate pointed at the desk chair. It was a standard office chair with the one addition of slight wings at the top. Something to rest your head against when tired or thinking. Knowing that they would just muddy the water if they stayed, Kate nodded her head in the door's direction at Colm. He followed her out.

Mrs Jessop was waiting on the landing, obviously unsure whether she should return to her office or check on the activities here. Colm gave a friendly wave and said to her, "Shall we return to your office, Mrs Jessop? We know you don't like leaving it unattended."

With a final look over her shoulder Mrs Jessop preceded them down the stairs. Kate called through to Edwards, "Mike, let me know what you find before you go."

Edwards was crouched over the desk chair and merely waved a hand in acknowledgement.

CHAPTER 7

Back in the reception office Colm was getting Mrs Jessop comfortable again with general chatter. Once they were all sat he flicked through his notebook and began. "Sorry about that interruption, Mrs Jessop. You were telling us about all the extra work you had to do to prepare for the special meeting."

"So much photocopying!"

"So did you attend this special meeting?" Kate asked.

"I attend all school meeting as minutes secretary," there was pride in Mrs Jessop's tone.

Again Colm nodded as though not surprised that she should be carrying out such an important role. He then lent forward, almost confidentially, "So how did this plan about the American college becoming involved in Blaiseforth go down? I am sure you are very observant and meticulous in your minute taking."

Mrs Jessop hesitated. Torn between seeming to gossip and her skill as the observer of the meeting. Finally she began, "Well, it was clear that Maisie Blaiseforth-Brown was not pleased."

Seeing their querying look, she elaborated, "Maisie is a member of the trustees and a member of the original Blaiseforth family."

"Was anyone else not too pleased?"

"Sir Kenneth Grant, he is the chair of the trustees, wanted to see more details about the educational impact of the American group. He used to be a leading figure in educational debates. I don't think he was for or against at the meeting."

"What about staff?"

"They were more restrained but..." she hesitated.

Again Colm lent forward, "Everything you tell us we will keep as confidential as we can."

That seemed to satisfy her and she continued, "I don't think Miss Sandford was happy about it. But it could have been that it was just sprung on them all and normally Miss Betteridge would discuss matters like this with her first."

Kate nodded in understanding before opening another route. "Would you say Miss Betteridge was well-liked by the staff?"

Again Mrs Jessop hesitated but then proceeded, "Well, Jackie Fleet, the Head of Literary Studies, has a bee in her bonnet about having Catherine Stanton's name re- written on the honours board."

Both Kate and Colm looked nonplussed. Mrs Jessop heaved a sigh at their ignorance, "Catherine Stanton, famous, or infamous, depending on your views," she said tartly, "lesbian writer in the 1940s? The trustees at the time removed her name from the board. Ms Fleet..." There was an emphasis on the Ms, "thinks it's time to rectify this situation."

"And Miss Betteridge didn't agree?" Kate queried, remembering the blank line she had seen when reading the board earlier.

"Well, in private she said she didn't mind one way or the other, she just disliked the way Ms Fleet was hounding her."

"Anyone else on Miss Betteridge's wrong side?" Colm prompted.

"There was the scene with Jude, Judith Chapman. She doesn't teach here, her husband Matthew does. Such a nice man." There was something in her tone that implied, unlike his wife.

"Judith Chapman?"

"It was all quite silly really. One of the upper sixth girls accused Matthew of inappropriate behaviour. All nonsense of course. She was miffed that he wouldn't give her a higher estimated grade for her university interviews. But Miss Betteridge said she had to be seen to be acting and investigating."

"So did she put him on gardening leave?"

"Not really. He wasn't to teach that particular girl's group at all and a teaching assistant chaperoned him in all his other classes. Just whilst Miss Betteridge investigated the girl's claim. Matthew seemed fine about it but that wasn't good enough for Jude Chapman. She came steaming up here demanding to see Miss Betteridge immediately." She looked towards the wall, which adjoined the Head's office. "I couldn't hear the words but she was very angry, Jude that is. You never saw Miss Betteridge angry. Then she, Jude, came storming out and shouting something like, 'You'll pay for this.'"

"If we could return to the night of Miss Betteridge's death," Kate said.

Mrs Jessop looked surprised at the change of direction but looked attentive.

"What time did you leave the school on that night? I assume you don't live in?"

"Goodness, no. I have a lovely little flat in Eashire itself. Broad Street."

"So what time did you get home?"

Mrs Jessop looked thoughtful. "Miss Betteridge said I should go after the special meeting concluded. She was taking Sir Kenneth and Maisie into her office. So it must have been just after five-thirty? Somewhere around then. I popped into the little grocers on Broad Street, so I think it must have been six-thirty by the time I got home."

"Do you live on your own, Mrs Jessop?" Colm asked kindly.

"Yes. Mr Jessop died several year's back."

"I'm sorry to hear that. So what did you do for the evening?"

"I made myself a bite to eat, ate in, washed up and sat down by eight to watch Bake Off. I do so love that programme."

Mrs Jessop jumped guiltily as the office door opened. Miss Sandford looked surprised to see Kate and Colm there.

"Was the meeting room not appropriate?"

"Absolutely fine," said Kate.

"We just didn't want to inconvenience Mrs Jessop by calling her away from her office," Colm said smoothly.

CHAPTER 8

Back in the meeting room Miss Sandford sat opposite them at one of the tables. She seemed a little unsettled to have found them talking with Mrs Jessop. She chewed her lip and then said, "Do take what Barbara says with a pinch of salt. She has been here too long and thinks we can't operate without her. In truth she was a good receptionist ten to twelve years ago but now she is out of her depth."

"Out of her depth?"

"For example, when we had the present IT system installed, Barbara had to have one of the juniors show her how to set her access up. Goodness knows how she will cope when she realises that if the American college get involved they will overhaul the entire system and put their own people in."

"Oh. Doesn't she realise this?"

"Probably, by now, because she was at the special meeting. It may not have occurred to her straight away but it must have sunk in by now."

"And will the American college plan go ahead?" Kate asked.

Miss Sandford sighed heavily, "I really don't know. It will depend on who the board appoints to succeed Elise and what their feelings are about the idea."

"Will you apply for the post?" Colm asked, smiling his smile.

She looked into the distance before replying, "No, I don't think I will. I am happy being the First Mate but I don't want to be the Captain."

"Could we go back to the evening after the special meeting?" Kate asked.

Miss Sandford nodded.

"What time did the meeting finish?"

"I think it was about five thirty-five. It couldn't have been much later because some of us needed to be in the refectory by five forty-five for the girls' supper."

"Was Miss Betteridge there as well?"

"No, she took Ken Grant and Maisie Brown into her office for further discussions. They are important people on the board. I think they were there for another half hour or so. Elise then had her supper with some of the other staff in the staff dining room and would then have retired to her sitting room."

"That was her usual routine?" Kate clarified, "but you don't know for sure that she actually did that Monday evening? Would anyone else have seen her during the evening?"

Miss Sandford nodded. "Yes, I am assuming that's what she did. The only person who would have seen her, for definite, would have been whichever lower sixth girl was due to serve her supper."

Kate raised a quizzical eyebrow and Miss

Sandford elaborated, "There is a rota. Each girl is allocated a date to prepare and serve Miss Betteridge her supper. It's normally a slice of cake and a mug of hot chocolate."

Kate's senses pricked. "So where is this supper prepared? In the main kitchen?"

"Oh no. The middle floor of this section of the school is given over to some staff accommodation and there is a small basic kitchen there, too. A bit like halls of residence in universities."

"So is it shop bought cake?" Colm asked.

"No. The cook keeps the tins stocked with homemade cakes and biscuits and the girls or staff alert her if any of the drinks stuff is running low. The girl is expected to slice the cake and make hot chocolate. Quite simple."

"Obviously we will want to talk to the girl who took Miss Betteridge her supper on Monday evening."

Miss Sandford nodded. "I will need to check the rota. Will she need an appropriate adult in attendance?"

"Not at this stage," replied Kate. We are just gathering basic information. We will not be interrogating her!" She smiled, in what she hoped was a friendly manner. She wasn't sure she succeeded.

CHAPTER 9

"Thoughts?"

Colm consulted his notebook, where he had been making copious notes. "Well it seems to me that several people had a gripe but nothing worth killing over."

Kate agreed. "List them out for me."

"According to Mrs Jessop, Maisie Blaiseforth-Brown was not happy about the American involvement but nothing has been firmed up so it seems a bit premature to kill Miss Betteridge so soon."

Kate looked thoughtful, "And of course Miss Sandford was not too pleased."

"Yes, but she doesn't want the Head's job to stop it."

"Or so she says."

Colm looked up. "You think she's lying?"

Kate thought before shaking her head, "No. I get the feeling she's telling the truth."

Colm suddenly brightened. "Do you think you could make ketamine in a school science lab?"

Kate looked at him. "Miss Sandford was teaching science. Maybe. There's a task for you. Use our friendly internet search engine and then ask Gus to point you in the direction of an appropriate colleague."

Second guessing himself Colm said, "It probably isn't that easy or everyone would be at it, wouldn't they?"

Kate shrugged her shoulders. "Who else have we got?"

"So then there is this Jackie Fleet and the name thing."

"Not worth murdering for, surely?"

"What about that chap's wife?"

"Again, unless there is more to it than we've been told, is it worth murdering for?"

"What about what Miss Sandford said about Mrs Jessop being out of her depth? Could she decide that killing off Miss Betteridge would allow her to keep her job?"

"Again it seems an extreme solution. And where would these people get the ketamine from?"

"You're not thinking it's the girl who served the supper, are you?" The astonishment was evident in Colm's tone.

"Not unless we can find a motive. And is a girl from Blaiseforth Manor going to be any more able to get a street drug?"

Colm grinned, "Actually, that might not be so far-fetched. Last year one of the Blaiseforth girls was caught up in a drugs raid on the Camworth Estate. Of course it was all quietly dealt with but..."

He left the idea hanging in the air. Kate nodded thoughtfully, "Umm. Yes with day girls as well as boarders, perhaps not so hard to come across."

"Okay I'm going to ring my desk phone and see who Bart has given us to do support work." The phone rang and rang and Kate was about to dial the main switchboard when it was picked up.

A breathless voice answered, "DI Medlar's desk, PC Giles here. How may I help you?"

"Alice? Has Bart assigned you to me?"

"Yes, ma'am."

Kate's heart lifted. Alice Giles was a bright and enthusiastic officer. "Okay I need the following info as soon as you can. A bio of Elise Betteridge and a look at her financial records. Then would you do a check on Elizabeth Sandford, Jackie or Jacqueline Fleet and Graham and Judith Chapman." Kate could hear the scratch of pen on paper as Alice took notes.

"Yes, ma'am. The bio is already on your desk and I'll get onto the finances straight away." There was no gloating in her voice at her pre-emptive task. As Kate knew: she was bright and enthusiastic.

"Great. We'll come back to the station before the close of play today."

Colm grinned and put a thumb up. "Alice is great."

Kate smiled and nodded. Bart had set her up with a small but perfectly formed team.

CHAPTER 10

Their discussion was interrupted by a brusque tap at the door and Miss Sandford stepped in, coaxing a girl before her. "This is Kitty Hardcastle." She then directed her attention to the girl and continued. "These people are asking some questions about Miss Betteridge's activities on Monday evening. Please answer as clearly as you can." With that she pointed Kitty towards a chair and she let herself out of the room.

Kate observed that the girl was at that awkward stage: on the cusp between child and woman. She wasn't tall but her legs seemed disproportionate to the rest of her. The word 'gangly' came to mind. Although wearing the school uniform there was a shabbiness about the girl; her collar was twisted under her jumper and the cuff on one arm hung unbuttoned below the jumper sleeve. Kitty let herself carefully into the chair and observed both police officers. Watching her face, Kate could see that there was an intelligence there and some curiosity.

Kate led. "Thank you for your time, Kitty."

The raised eyebrow that social nicety received told Kate more than any form of words and she eased back on the soft soap. "You were on the rota to take Miss Betteridge her supper tray on Monday evening, is that correct?"

"It is but I didn't do it."

For a moment Kate was unsure if this was a negative confession but Kitty continued. She began to speak quickly using her arms and hands to clarify her words. Kitty's hands lightly tapped her thighs. "You see Ms Fleet decided that we were not being attentive enough in class and set us a text analysis for that night to be handed in first thing Tuesday and I lost my text."

Kate and Colm both looked confused. "Well no-one could let me have a copy of the text until they had done the assignment but by the time someone had finished I didn't have time to do the assignment and take Old Betty, sorry, Miss Betteridge her supper, so Izzy, Isabelle Grey, said she'd do it for me."

"So we need to speak to Izzy Grey about Monday's supper tray?"

Kitty nodded. "Do you want me to go and get her? She's in my class now."

"Yes, thank you, but would you not talk to her about what we want to ask her, please?"

"Yes of course." Kitty rose and moved towards the door.

"Did you find your missing text?" Colm asked.

Kitty laughed. "Yes. I had packed it up with the thesaurus I had been using. When I went into class on Tuesday it was there on the shelf."

As the door shut Colm turned to Kate, "Could this Izzy have planned for Kitty's text to go missing?"

"It seems a bit far-fetched. Come to that what would any pupil have against a teacher to want to murder them?"

"Oh, I dunno. I hated a few at my school," Colm half joked.

"Yes, don't we all have those in our cupboards. But hate enough to kill..?"

"Perhaps her death has nothing to do with the school."

"We'll have to check her social life, but do you think the staff who live in have much of a life outside the school?"

Further discussion was stopped by a firm but gentle knock on the door. Kate called Izzy Grey in. A young woman entered. She was neat and compact, smiled and headed for the chair opposite Kate and Colm. Kate wondered if she had had as much poise when she was this age. She somehow doubted it. Izzy sat and waited attentively.

"Isabelle Grey?" Kate asked.

A surprisingly deep, rich voice answered, "Please call me Izzy. People only use Isabelle when I am in trouble." A smile accompanied this last part.

"Are you in trouble much?" asked Colm giving her one of his warm smiles and leaning forward.

Kate noted that Izzy's shoulders dropped and she adopted a more positive pose towards Colm.

She decided to let Colm take the lead and relaxed back into her chair to give him the signal.

Colm made a point of looking at his notebook before saying, "According to Kitty you kindly did her rota duty to take Miss Betteridge her supper tray. Is that correct?"

Izzy sighed gently, "Poor Kitty. She's always losing things and Monday it was her lit text. We were in fear of death not to have completed the assignment. Kitty was in such a state so I said I would do it."

Kate noted that a hanky had appeared in Izzy's hands and she was torturing it into twisted shapes. Perhaps not quite so poised.

"So what does taking Miss Betteridge her supper entail?" Colm continued.

"You take her a slice of cake and a mug of hot chocolate."

"Have you done this before?"

"Yes, at the beginning of term it was my turn. I think we get about three evenings across the term."

"Is there a choice of cake or do you just serve whatever's in the cake tin?"

"I think it's whatever's in the tin."

"So you sliced a piece of cake?"

"No," said Izzy. "The tray was already set up. Kitty must have got it ready when she was waiting for one of us to finish."

"Do you know Kitty set the tray ready? Did you ask her?"

Izzy paused and looked perplexed. "Well, no. I just assumed that she had because everything was ready."

"Describe what was on the tray. Was it a round or square tray?"

"It's sort of oblong, with handles at each end. It's quite heavy, even when it's empty."

Colm nodded encouragingly.

"The cake plate was to the right. It looked like Kit... whoever cut it had had problems because I think there was sort of a slice and some large crumbs. It was covered in plastic wrap. There was a napkin folded in the middle and then a mug with chocolate granules in the bottom and a sugar bowl to the left."

Izzy appeared to be checking the details in her mind's eye and then slowly nodded.

"So how did you make the hot chocolate?" Kate interceded.

Izzy switched her gaze to Kate, almost surprised that she was also in the room. "Kitty... I mean someone, had left the milk in a plastic jug ready to go into the microwave, so I heated it up and poured it into the mug and stirred it."

Colm came back in, "Did Miss Betteridge ask why you were there rather than Kitty?"

"I'm not sure she knew who was on the rota," said Izzy. "And any way she didn't turn to look at me when I went into her room. She was working at her desk with her back to the door. I put the tray on the table and left."

"So what time did you deliver Miss Betteridge her supper?"

Izzy paused. "I left the common room just before seven, so…"

Kate could see her working the times out in her head, "by the time I'd warmed the milk I suppose about seven-fifteen."

Kate was unsure what to ask next. Assuming Miss Betteridge had her supper whilst the chocolate was hot, her time of death must have been around nine-fifteen.

Colm was still pursuing an idea, "Who clears away the tray? Miss Betteridge?"

Izzy's laugh held a note of scorn. "No. Normally whoever takes the supper in collects it about an hour later."

"But you didn't?" queried Colm.

Izzy frowned, "No, one of the other girls said they would do it but I can't remember who."

Kate was alert. Could this be their killer after all? One of the girls?

"Think back, Izzy, this could be really important. Who offered to go back to the sitting room?"

The tortured hanky seemed about to be sundered, "I... I really can't remember. I think several girls offered. No-one minds helping Kitty out. I'm really sorry."

Tears threatened on the edge of her eyelids but did not fall.

"Don't worry," added Colm in his calm

voice. "At this stage we are just gathering facts. Everything you have told us so far is very useful."

Izzy smiled weakly.

Colm closed his notebook and smiled back at her. "Thank you, Izzy. You have been very clear and concise. We'll let you get back to class."

CHAPTER 11

Izzy left with a backward glance at Colm. "I think you have a hit there," Kate smiled.

Colm blushed but further talk was prevented by the arrival of Mrs Jessop wheeling, what Kate thought, was a hostess trolley. "Its lunchtime and you haven't stopped for a break since you arrived so I have arranged some sandwiches." With a flourish she took out a plateful together with some cake slices. "There's a choice of tea or coffee."

"Mrs Jessop that is very thoughtful of you. Thank you so much."

Mrs Jessop blushed at Colm's kind words as he continued, "Would you like to join us for lunch? The school must allow you a lunch break!"

"I... er," then she visibly made a decision, "would love to. I'll just go and collect my packed lunch and mug." She hastened out of the door.

Kate raised a questioning eyebrow. "I thought we might get a little more gossip out of her. Find out some background?" Colm suggested.

Kate nodded and Mrs Jessop returned. Colm busied himself making drinks and soon they were sat around one of the tables. Kate was not surprised to see that Mrs Jessop's lunch box contained neatly wrapped foil parcels, which she unwrapped carefully, avoiding tearing the foil. Kate wondered if they were for reuse.

Colm began conversationally, "Had Miss Betteridge been headteacher for long?"

Mrs Jessop was chewing, so shook her head. Once the morsel had been swallowed she said, "Oh, no. She was only appointed seven years ago."

"So you have known how many Heads?" Kate asked.

"It was Miss Gillespie when I first arrived, she was in poor health and the trustees made the decision to replace her. I don't think she'd have gone willingly. Very much of the old school," she gave a knowing look and added, "Die in harness, type."

Kate nodded in understanding. Where did a single, life-long teacher in a boarding school go when they retired?

"Then it was Dr Wingfield. Now she was a new broom." There was a note of admiration in her tone. "She opened up the school to the day girls. She wanted the school to be more a part of the shire, 'not an alien squatting here'." Her voice deepened as she quoted from her former employer. Mrs Jessop continued, "She introduced new subjects, like IT, sociology and psychology. I forget what else, but she really got the school moving into the twenty-first century."

"That must have meant a lot of work for

you," Colm said sympathetically.

Mrs Jessop nodded her agreement, "But I was younger then. Took it more in my stride."

Colm looked enquiringly at her and she continued, "I had never worked with computers before. I managed when Dr Wingfield installed the first school computer system but then Miss Betteridge introduced a far more complicated one. I was so worried about it. I even thought I may have to retire but little Izzy Grey came to my rescue."

Kate's eyebrows shot into her fringe, "Isabelle Grey."

"Yes, poor mite. She's an orphan. I'm not sure of the details but I think her parents died in a traffic accident. So she was then taken in by a great aunt who died quite suddenly just before Izzy came to us. Fortunately, the aunt had made arrangements in her will for a fund of some kind that would pay her school and university fees until she is twenty-one. I don't know if there are no other relatives, or just no-one who wanted responsibility for an eleven year old, so most holidays she stays in school. Some of the girls invite her home for a break but she spends most of her time here and she sort of, gravitated towards me."

"A bit of a mother figure," Colm said knowingly.

Mrs Jessop gave a little laugh, "Maybe." And

blushed again.

"So how did Izzy rescue you?" Kate tried to make it a conversational question rather than an interrogative one.

Mrs Jessop took it at face value, "Well, Izzy is a genius when it comes to computers. She even persuaded Miss Betteridge to put programming in the syllabus. She hopes to go to Oxbridge to do computer sciences."

"Ah," said Colm knowingly, "she helped you with the new systems?"

Mrs Jessop nodded, "She did, and does. Every so often she comes in and checks my system is running properly, de-frags it and other stuff." It was obvious that she didn't have a clue what Izzy did with her computer and the system.

Eager to underline how helpful Izzy was she continued. "She often pops in and helps me with admin. Why only Monday evening when I had all that photocopying to do and then Miss Betteridge wanted it put into the posh files that the American college had left. It would have taken me hours but Izzy popped her head round the door, saw I was snowed under and came in and helped."

Not wanting to appear to be over thinking this information, Kate changed the subject and asked, "Was Maisie Blaiseforth-Brown here when you were?"

"Oh no. But her daughter, Clare was. She left," she stopped to work out time lines, "three years ago. Nice girl. Nice family. No airs and graces." Not like some, was the unspoken criticism.

Colm broke in, "What sort of person was Miss Betteridge? You must have worked very closely with her."

Mrs Jessop nodded eagerly, "We did." She paused, thinking about how she wanted to express her opinion, "She was a perfectionist. She was determined that Blaiseforth Manor would be one of the best public schools in the country."

"So the American college idea was not a real surprise then?" Colm hazarded a guess.

Mrs Jessop looked thoughtful before admitting, "No not really."

"Does Miss Betteridge have any family or friends that we could speak to?" Kate asked.

"I don't know about family but she would regularly visit Miss Hazel. She's an ex teacher. She must be well into her nineties by now. She taught Miss Betteridge when she was a pupil."

"Is she local?"

"Oh yes. She's at The Orchard in Witcham."

"Is she..." Kate tailed off. At ninety something was she compos mentis?

Guessing Kate's direction of thought, Mrs Jessop laughed, "She's as sharp as a pin. Always has been." She paused, "I'm not sure if anyone has thought to tell her of Miss Betteridge's passing."

A bell sounded and Mrs Jessop sighed as she

carefully repacked her lunch box with the now empty foil and drained the last of the tea from her mug. "No rest for the wicked," she smiled as she left.

CHAPTER 12

As Mrs Jessop left she passed Edwards in the doorway. He held it open for her as she moved through. He looked longingly at the plates of food. Kate took pity, "Help yourself Mike."

With a second look he said, "Nah. Me and the team will pick up something on our way back."

"Anything in the room?" Kate asked optimistically.

"Not a lot," said Edwards. "We picked up some fingerprints off the back of the chair, near the wings but other than that it was clean. They obviously have better cleaners than we do at the station!" he said with a wry smile.

Kate sighed. "Check with Gus about our victim's prints and see what we've got left."

Edwards nodded. "We've bagged her laptop and mobile but didn't find any other electronic devices."

"Okay, I'll check with the staff here."

"Having been given the run down by Bart we also targeted the kitchenette on the landing. Here we found more prints but still I think the cleaners have been in there. We're assuming that's where her supper was prepared?"

"Yes. But anyone could have had access. I'll talk to the staff about whose prints should be in there."

"Okay then. I'll get our results back to you asap."

"Thanks, Mike." He waved as he left and Kate got a glimpse of his team taking out their equipment.

Kate breathed out heavily. "So not a lot of forensics. Not a lot of motive. I think we need to talk with Miss Sandford again. We'll go up to the room and let her talk us through it again."

***

Miss Sandford paused outside the sturdy wooden door and half raised her hand as though to knock and then laughed at herself. She opened the door but stepped back to allow Kate and Colm to precede her into the room.

Kate took more time to look at the room. Miss Sandford hovered by the open door, seemingly reluctant to come further into the room. Kate turned to her and said, "I'm assuming that she was found in this chair," indicating the desk chair.

Miss Sandford nodded but didn't move from her post by the door.

"Could you show me how Miss Betteridge was seated?"

Miss Sandford looked aghast but came to the desk. Reluctantly she pulled the chair out on its casters and sat in it. She closed her eyes and began to arrange herself in the chair. Head against the left wing. Left arm slipped down between the arm and her body. The right was flung out across the arm rest. "I can't remember how her legs were," she said as she opened her eyes. "I only remember the top part of her."

"That's fine. Thank you. Were her eyes closed?"

"Yes. That's why I thought she was sleeping."

Kate looked around the room. "Is this how you found the room when you came in on Wednesday morning?"

Miss Sandford also looked round. "Yes. Well, apart from the dust!"

"What about the curtains and lights?" Colm asked.

"Oh, yes. The curtains were drawn and there was only the desk lamp on. I think that enforced the idea that she had fallen asleep working the previous night."

Kate nodded. She spotted another door in the opposite corner from the entrance. "Where does that lead?"

"Into Miss Betteridge's bedroom and bathroom."

Kate walked across and opened the door. A small foyer, with two other doors off it was revealed. Kate looked in the room opposite. This was the bedroom. Everything was in very pale wood, making the dark fingerprint powder even more obvious. It didn't look like forensics had found a great deal here either. Kate felt the room was clinical: the only real colour was the midnight blue duvet set on the bed. She wandered over to the dressing table and looked in the drawers. Underwear, scarves but no private diary or address book. She also tried the bedside cabinets but they were equally impersonal.

The bathroom was small, clean and modern. Apart from the standard bottles of shampoo and body wash there was little to give flesh to Miss Betteridge's personality. Did she like pine fresh shampoo or was that the nearest one to hand when she shopped? Or was it what the school provided?

Back in the sitting room she noted that Colm was going through the drawers of the large desk. "Anything? A diary? An address book?"

Colm shook his head. Miss Sandford, who had taken up her post by the door again, cleared her throat. "It may well be on her laptop."

"Did she have a mobile or any other electronic devices?"

"Her mobile should be on her desk." Miss Sandford's eyes searched the desktop looking for the item. "I don't think she had an ipad or anything like it. Just the mobile and the laptop."

"Don't worry," said Colm, we have taken the laptop and mobile in for examination. We will issue a receipt, of course."

CHAPTER 13

Back on the landing, Kate pointed to the other doors. "Who else lives on this floor?"

Miss Sandford pointed to the door opposite, "Miss Clements, Modern Languages lives there." She turned and pointed to the left, Miss Hooper, Art and Sculpture and Dr Heath," pointing right, "is there."

"So the end door is the kitchen?" Colm asked.

Miss Sandford nodded.

"Does everyone on this floor have access to it?"

Miss Sandford nodded again. "Yes. I know Dr Heath. Margery often prefers to make herself tea and toast rather than the main supper in the dining room. And the others would have, at least, made themselves hot drinks."

Kate walked into the kitchen pulling on gloves. It was a windowless, small box room. One side had a preparation area, barely big enough for a bread board, a two slice toaster and a microwave. Above was a cupboard. Kate opened the doors and peered inside. One half had the necessary elements for a range of hot drinks and the other held a selection of cake tins. The other side of the room had a sink, a fridge and another cupboard, which on investigation, held crockery.

Kate returned to the first cupboard. There

were several brands of hot chocolate. "Would Miss Betteridge have a specific brand of hot drink?"

"The blue container is hers. She actually ordered it from France."

"So no-one else would think to use it."

Miss Sandford smiled, "Not a chance!"

Kate indicated to Colm to bag the jar. "What about sugar? Did she take sugar in her hot chocolate?"

Miss Sandford nodded. "Yes and she always insisted on it being in a sugar bowl. That one there." She indicated a small green lidded pot. Kate had assumed it was a jam pot but on taking it down and removing the lid found, as told, the sugar. Again Kate handed it to Colm for bagging.

"Do you know which tin contains the cake Miss Betteridge would have eaten on Monday evening?"

Miss Sandford hesitated. "I think it was whatever was in the tins."

Kate pulled out all the cake tins and opened each one. The second tin contained the remains of a fruit cake, whereas the other two had biscuits and a sponge in. "Bag this as well, Colm."

Miss Sandford asked the question that had been hovering in the air since Kate began to go through the cupboard. "Do you think she was poisoned?"

"It is a possibility we are looking at," Kate said non-committedly.

"But... But..." Miss Sandford gathered her thoughts. "If it was in the sugar or cake the poison could have been for anyone."

"That is a possibility but in the light of all the evidence we have we think Miss Betteridge was the intended target."

Kate remembered that Izzy had said the items on the pre-prepared tray had been covered in plastic wrap but she couldn't detect any in the kitchenette. Had the killer removed it?

Colm changed the subject, "Who has access to this floor. We're assuming that the kitchen is not locked?"

"No. The kitchen is open to anyone and this floor is only supposed to be the residents and whichever lower sixth is on duty but it is not policed. If the person came to this floor they must have been very brazen; who knows when one of the mistresses would come out and see them."

It was obvious that Miss Sandford thought the perpetrator was an outsider. Kate did not disabuse her of the idea. Taking one further look at the small room she turned to leave, glancing at her watch as she did so. Kate turned to Miss Sandford, "May I have a list of the names and addresses of the trustees, please and an indication of which ones attended the Monday meeting."

"Yes of course." She strode away towards the stairs. Kate turned to Colm. "Would you check the school rubbish bins and see if you can find the film wrap. There's none here but Izzy said the cake was covered."

Colm made a face. "Yes, boss."

"There is a paper suit in my car if you need it."

Colm looked at Kate and then down at himself, "Not sure a small is going to cover more than one leg, boss."

On their way back to reception Colm peeled off to the back of the school and Kate continued on to meet up with Miss Sandford in the foyer. "We would like to talk to the staff that live in the other rooms on the landing. When would be convenient tomorrow?"

Miss Sandford sighed. Perhaps she had thought that the one visit would be it. "The girls have classes tomorrow morning but the afternoon is given over to sports and hobbies. I am sure that will be a convenient time."

"I'm assuming Mr Chapman doesn't live in?"

Miss Sandford shook her head.

"What about Ms Fleet?"

Miss Sandford shook her head again.

"In that case I will need their home addresses, please."

CHAPTER 14

It was only a few minutes later that Colm joined her in her car. "Sorry, boss. Bin collection is first thing Tuesday morning. Anything thrown away Monday night had gone. I did talk to the head cook who said that a roll should be there and that it was quite a new one."

"Damn! Do you think that's coincidence or that we have a well-planned murder?"

"I'm not sure. It all seems to stem from Kitty losing her book. Could that have been planned?"

"But the book was only important because Ms Fleet had set them an assignment to be done that evening."

"So are we saying that Ms Fleet is our killer?"

"It seems far-fetched but we rule nothing out at this stage."

Colm asked, "What next, boss?"

"Organise some extra uniforms to do initial interviews with all the staff over the weekend. And make sure they take digital fingerprints at the same time. That will help forensics." Kate paused thinking about Bart's 'tread carefully' comment. "That will prove least disruptive to the school. Designate Alice to co-ordinate and flag up anything of interest."

"Anything in particular you want them to focus on?"

"No. Get their ideas of the victim and where they were on the night in question. I'd like to have a look at Ms Fleet's and Mrs Chapman's and we'll do the three on the landing that Miss Sandford mentioned."

Colm was making notes. "I'm not sure how many we have in tomorrow but at least Eashire Rovers is playing away."

"Okay, now we'll go back to the morgue so you can collect your car and if Gus is still around ask him about the production of ketamine or ask him who to ask."

Colm nodded. "Do you think it's the ketamine that's going to lead us to the murderer?"

"Well, at the moment we can't seem to find a motive big enough to kill for. Who's your best source for drugs?"

Straight-faced Colm asked, "It depends what you're after. Boss?"

Kate poked out her tongue and smiled. "Funny! Is there anyone you can ask about the drugs in Eashire? I know we're not immune from the drug problem here but ketamine seems to be a strange drug to use."

Colm agreed. Driving back to the morgue they went over again their possible suspects and once again felt that no-one had motive enough. "We're going to have to do some more digging into Miss Betteridge. There must be something in her life that warranted her death." Kate said more with hope than conviction.

Back in the morgue car park Colm asked, "I'll follow you back to the station and organise the guys in blue."

"Guys?"

"Yeh. Guys can mean females as well."

"Not sure about that. Anyway I'll see you there. I've got to talk to Bart about how far we haven't got. But after that I want to gather the team and start putting information on the boards. Give me half-an-hour with Bart."

***

Twenty minutes later Kate was sat in DCI Bartholomew's office giving him an update of the day's events. "So, in short, no obvious suspects?"

Kate shook her head, "No, sir. DC Hunter is trying to track the ketamine."

"I agree it is an unusual choice of drug, so you may get lucky. What are your plans?"

"Tomorrow I want to talk with some of the trustees and the staff who live on the same floor as Miss Betteridge. Someone may have heard something…" It sounded lame to Kate's own ears but Bart nodded.

"You know to tread carefully, don't you Kate?"

"Yes, sir"

"But carefully does not mean ignoring anything. Everything is to be done by the book. If you need access to anyone who is proving..." he paused, "unavailable, let me know and I will clear a path."

"Thank you sir."

"What is it they say, 'Love or money are the likeliest motives? I suggest you follow the money, Kate. A place like Blaiseforth Manor is awash with the stuff but it doesn't mean that someone doesn't want more."

Transcript Audio Log 1min 13secs

At lunchtime the school was salivating over the news that the police were in and had been talking to staff and pupils. Someone said she'd also seen a forensics team, in their white all in ones, heading for Betty's room. No-one has yet mentioned the reason why but it won't take them long to start talking about the nature of Betty's death.

I wondered what could have alerted them to something suspicious but it seems that there was an autopsy. Is that usual? I thought if there were no obvious signs of misadventure they would have settled for the original supposition that it was a heart attack. I wonder what the autopsy revealed. There didn't seem to be any outward signs on her body. I did check. I wonder if they analysed her stomach contents.

I understand that they can pinpoint death very well if they analyse what was last eaten.

But I'm not worried. I know I've covered my tracks well. The bins were emptied Tuesday morning and I wore gloves. I wore gloves to start with but I took them off for the film wrap. Did I put them back on? I can't remember. I'm sure I did. Anyway I made sure I didn't touch anything. Not that the police will find very much. I know because I know the domestic team have been up there. I overheard one of them saying that it didn't feel right cleaning when she, I assume Miss Betteridge, had gone.

I'm sure there is no link with me but I will hide the ketamine where no-one will dream of looking.

I saw the police as they were leaving this afternoon. I don't know which of them is in charge but the man looks like a farmer and the woman is small and unremarkable. But she did look like she had sharp eyes. I don't think they'll bother me.

CHAPTER 15

Back in room eleven Kate found her team assembled. Sergeant Hughes and Alice were putting pictures and information on their murder board. Colm was at his computer. "The uniforms are all set up for tomorrow and I have arranged with Miss Sandford that the interviews can take place in the meeting room. It will accommodate seven officers."

"Thanks, Colm, what are you up to now?"

"Umm. Just tapping up one of the drugs boys and then I have a bit of info for you."

"Okay, well let's have everyone together and we'll see what we've got." Kate moved to the front of the room. Sergeant Hughes was a long service police officer. Probably should have gone up the career ladder but seemed content where he was. Kate knew him to be respected amongst his colleagues and so she was pleased to have him on the team.

"Thanks, Alice, that's great. Do we have another uniform with us?"

Alice stepped back from the board and turned but before she could answer, a voice behind Kate said, "Yes ma'am. That would be me."

Kate's heart sank but she turned and smiled a welcome, "Len, that's great!"

PC Len Goodfellow. If ever someone was misnamed it was Len. His colleagues made jokes about his sloping shoulders when it came to work or blame. Kate had also heard some of his remarks about race and gays. He was like something out of the ark. And it wasn't like he was that old. Hughes would retire before Len did. Inwardly Kate shrugged. Well three out of four were good odds in a team.

Colm joined her at the board. The others took their seats. Between them Colm and Kate took them through Gus' findings and their time at the school. Then Alice gave a quick breakdown of the victim and her finances. "Nothing looks dodgy or unexpected. She has a mortgage on a cottage in Eashire that she lets for most of the year. I suppose that's her retirement home. Other than that, very little expenditure each month and so a healthy savings account but nothing that can't be accounted for."

"So, any suggestions for motive for our victim's murder?" Kate said to the room at large.

"What about her love life?" Len queried. That would have been a fine observation Kate thought if he hadn't accompanied it with a leer.

Alice answered, "There's nothing obvious in what I have found so far. But I'll keep digging."

Colm cleared his throat and puffed his chest, he had news! "Gus thinks he may have found what she was suffocated with."

Kate was alert, "Do tell."

"Film wrap!"

"What? The stuff you wrap your sandwiches in?" Len asked.

Colm nodded. "Gus said he found a small piece trapped in the oesophagus. He's not confirming it as the means because he says that she may have chewed it off something and unknowingly inhaled it but when pushed he agreed that was unlikely."

Kate sat and leant back in her chair and closed her eyes, "So someone entered the room once she was drugged and what... wrapped her face in film wrap?"

"Well, Gus thinks she was barely conscious from the ketamine so it wouldn't have been that hard. Just wrap her whole head in it."

"That sounds so... hands on. Two different ways of killing. The ketamine, which is long distant so the consequences are not seen but then close up and personal with the film wrap."

"You're not suggesting two killers, are you?" Colm's voice was shocked.

"No," said Kate. "I don't think so but it's just so different. Why the film wrap? Gus thinks the ketamine alone would have done the job."

"They had to be sure she was dead?" Colm suggested.

Kate ran her fingers through her hair. "Right, we've all had a full day. I'd like to reconvene at eight thirty tomorrow. Alice would you let uniforms know that I want to brief them at the same time?" In the meantime let your little grey cells have some exercise."

Alice nodded as everyone but Colm filed out. "Are you off home as well, boss?"

"Not directly. I need to do some shopping. I had green toast for breakfast!"

Colm laughed and wrinkled his nose. "Okay boss, see you in the morning."

CHAPTER 16

Food shopping accomplished, Kate sat down with a supermarket rice and curry. Gus had sent through his full autopsy report and photographs and Kate read through as she ate. It did occur to her that food and the report would seem a highly unlikely pairing to others but she could read the information with a detachment that did not affect her appetite. There was nothing new in the report, apart from the mention of the film wrap. Could you match a piece of film wrap to a particular make or even roll? She'd ask Gus at some point.

So where had the wrap come from? Had their killer used what was there in the kitchenette and then taken it away with them? It was a feasible scenario but the bins had been collected long before they knew it was a crime.

Kate's email alert sounded on her phone. She grabbed for it eagerly. Perhaps Colm had got some intel about the ketamine. Her face fell when she realised it was from Robin. Should she just delete it before reading it? It would be more of the same.

"It doesn't have to be like this."

Yes it did. What was wrong with a clean break? Or was it because, for once, she had been the activator? Is that what Robin was struggling with? The Eashire job had come up at just the right time and for once she had done what she wanted. No, more desperate than that. She had done what she needed to do. Her finger hovered over the delete button but then she gave in. Robin might actually have something important to say.

"Hi Kate. Taking a break next week and thought I'd pop by Eashire. Could we meet for a coffee and a chat? I could come to the station. Let me know asap. Robin xx"

Kate cringed. Robin coming to Eashire? And was that a threat, "I could come to the station"? Oh this was all she needed right in the middle of her first independent murder enquiry. What had they to chat about? They'd had a relationship. It hadn't worked out. They split. End of story. But she didn't need Robin turning up at the station.

"Hi Robin. Not sure why we need to meet and chat. I thought we had said all we needed last time we saw each other. Eashire holds little for a relaxing break so why not go somewhere else for your break? Kate."

Kate worried over the wording. Should she just write a flat refusal? But she didn't trust Robin not to turn up at the station and put on a little show. She sent the text. By now her curry had congealed and she found her appetite diminished. Scraping the remains of her supper into the food recycling bin and her plate into the sink, she picked up Alice's report and went through to the sitting room. Her one concession to luxury was the large sofa that took up most of the room. She sprawled and tried to let her shoulders relax. The knots refused to release. Damn Robin!

As though psychic her mobile announced the arrival of an email. Kate hadn't realised that she had been holding her breath as she looked at the name of the sender. It was Colm. Breathing out she read his message.

"Hi Boss. Can we meet at the Prince Street station tomorrow? 7.30am? We need to speak with one of the drugs team. Colm."

It sounded like Colm had a lead on the ketamine. Brilliant. She replied with a single "Yes."

She was beginning to think they would never get a thread to come loose with this murder. Perhaps the ketamine would open the case up. Before she'd had time to think further the email alert sounded again. This time it was Robin's reply.

"Don't be like that, Kate. You can't abandon five years in one argument. Please meet me for a drink. I intend to be coming through Eashire next Tuesday. Just one drink? Please. I promise I won't contact you again after we have talked once more. Robin xx"

Kate put her head in her hands. Was she really going to have to deal with Robin again? She knew in her heart of hearts that she was. Sighing deeply she began the reply:

"If you haven't already organised accommodation the Golden Lion is a C17th coaching inn. The rooms are lovely and they have a good chef."

Kate knew about the Golden Lion because she stayed there when she'd come for the Eashire interview. She also knew that Robin would want somewhere with a decent menu.

"I'll meet you in the bar, Tuesday evening at 7pm. Kate"

At least Kate knew she'd be able to get a pot of tea there at that time of night. It wasn't that Kate was teetotal by conviction. A couple of years back she'd had a very serious infection to the point where the doctor had talked about hospitalisation. She'd avoided that but had been on antibiotics for three weeks. Obviously she'd not been allowed to drink alcohol in that time and when she was allowed it didn't taste right. She found that she could still enjoy a night out: it was more about a state of mind than the alcohol. One time a colleague had slipped vodka into an orange juice and she could taste the alcohol. Later she talked to him and said his action was akin to using GHB. He had been horrified: she had been furious.

Another email message. Short and not so sweet.

"Thanks for the info about the Golden Lion. See you Tuesday. Robin xx"

Kate felt she could feel Robin gloating through the ether. Damn! She opened Alice's report and tried to occupy her mind with the life and times of Elise Betteridge. It was a worthy but unremarkable life. The post at Blaiseforth had been the crowning glory in a life of teaching. She was well respected in the world of education and had a reputation of being focused on the importance of education for girls.

At the end of an hour Kate closed the file, yawned and stretched. Not a hint, even a shadow that they could chase in relation to her death. If Kate had to draw up a list of people least likely to be murdered, Elise Betteridge would be in the top five. What had they missed?

CHAPTER 17

Kate had not slept well but it did mean that she was more than ready to get going the following morning. Prince Street police station was no longer a walk in station but Eashire's small drugs team worked out of the back of it. Kate spotted Colm as she drove into the car park at the back of the station. He was talking to a young man in jeans with the obligatory rips across the knees, a sweatshirt and worn leather jacket. To Kate he looked ridiculously young.

Walking across the Tarmac, Colm called out, "Morning boss."

As she got closer he made the introductions, "DC Terry Gilbert, this is DI Kate Medlar."

Kate held out her hand and met a rough palmed and firm hand shake.

"This way then," said Terry turning to a digital keypad and punching in a series of numbers. On the final beep the door clicked and Terry pushed it open. They followed him down a fusty corridor painted that institutional green that reminded Kate of the Victorian built junior school she had attended. Terry led them into an open plan office. A few desks were occupied but most weren't. As Terry walked past an empty one he grabbed a chair and indicated that Colm do the same. Soon they were huddled round a computer. Terry was in between Kate and Colm and navigated the computer's workings.

"Right, here we go. I thought I'd remembered right." Terry leant back in his chair and pointed at the screen. From their respective angles Kate and Colm could make out very little. "Talk us through it, mate," said Colm.

"Yeh, of course." He leant forward and began to relay the information. "The eleventh of last month Neil Turner, a vet, was broken into. Well, his practice was. He doesn't live above the shop." He leant back again and addressed Kate, "To be honest, the security was not what it could have been. Turner's selling out to a larger company, economies of scale, apparently, so he hadn't kept everything as shipshape as he should have."

"Anyway they cleared him out of everything." He chuckled, "I imagine some gullible sod is going to be sold worming tablets as the latest high!" He went back to the screen, "But the thing I remembered was that they took three phials of liquid ketamine. Meant for injection, not oral consumption.

"So has any of the stock turned up on the street?" Colm asked.

"We've had a couple of hits and are following leads, but nothing about the ketamine."

"So do you know who's behind it?" Kate inquired.

"We have an idea but it's getting the evidence. His name is Gary Phipps on the

Camworth Estate."

"Is it worth our going to see him?" Kate probed.

Terry shook his head vigorously, "No," and then as an afterthought, "Ma'am".

Colm grinned. "Don't worry Ter, we'll keep out of your hair. Won't we boss?" He looked directly at Kate and she got the message.

"Of course but can we have an interview if you do get him in? Or let us know if you get any intel about the ketamine?"

"Yes. My boss is out following up something now so if it pans out I'll talk with him and explain the situation."

Kate rose. "Thanks, Terry. This may be an important lead for us."

Shaking hands all round, Terry led them back out to the car park.

As the door closed Kate said, "Well done, Colm. Let's hope they get enough of a lead that'll help us. Now did you bring your car?"

"No, I walked from my flat."

"Good. You can drive. To the station first and then we're going to visit the great and good of Eashire. At least you'll know the way."

CHAPTER 18

Room eleven was crowded with uniformed bodies. Kate saw Alice at the front giving out copies of the staffing list she'd collected from Mrs Jessop. As she made her way to the front, the noise in the room abated and all turned to look at Kate. She turned to face them and smiled. "Thanks everyone for being so prompt. DC Colm will talk you through your task today." Kate sat on the edge of a table and Colm strode to the front.

"Okay, we have an unexplained death at Blaiseforth Manor. Miss Elise Betteridge, the headteacher, was found dead Tuesday morning but is believed to have died between nine and ten on the Monday evening."

Kate noted that everyone but Len was writing the basic info in their notebooks.

"You are conducting the preliminary interviews so we need to know where they were at that time on Monday. In addition we want to know something of the school dynamics. You've all got IDENT1 kits so fingerprint as you go"

Kate noticed a few puzzled frowns and added, "Things like had anyone fallen out with our victim. What did they think of her, as a person, as a Head."

Colm nodded. "I've arranged with the acting

head that you can use the meetings room. The interviews can go on simultaneously." Colm turned to Alice. "If you keep the master staffing list and make sure everyone in school today is interviewed."

Alice nodded.

Colm continued, "Tom and Karen, you can visit the staff that live off site. There's only half a dozen that won't be in school today." Two PCs nodded and Kate was able to identify them. They looked intelligent and enthusiastic.

"What about the kids?" It was Len Goodfellow.

Kate answered, "For the time being we will not be interviewing the pupils on mass. If anyone does need an interview, DC Hunter and I will conduct them."

Len shrugged. Kate wondered if it was a good idea to let Len loose in Blaiseforth at all. What could she give him to do to keep him in the station? It came to her. "Len I'd like you to remain here and to dig up everything you can on the American college our victim was planning to go into business with. Find out what their reputation is, who the key players are. That sort of thing."

Kate was unsure whether Len was pleased or not with his special assignment but it made her feel easier that he was not going to be interacting with the staff at the school.

"Any questions?" Colm asked.

One of the officers, burning with youth and energy, "What should we do if we think we've got something important in our interview?"

"Talk with PC Giles... Alice. She's going to be co-ordinating all your interviews. So anything, no matter how small, flag it up to her as you hand in your sheets. Okay then, off you go. There's a minibus for the school team."

There was a murmuring of voices as they gathered their equipment and began to leave the room but Kate could not detect any dissent in its tones.

"And make sure your handwriting is legible," Colm called after them.

Laughter greeted this final sally. Silence filled the room. "Thanks, Colm. Good briefing."

Colm nodded. "So where are we off to today?"

Kate consulted her own notes and said. "Let's go and talk to Maisie Blaiseforth-Brown and Sir Kenneth Grant, since our victim was most keen to win them over.

CHAPTER 19

Maisie Blaisefoth-Brown lived in Westergate. According to Colm it was a Victorian extension to medieval Eashire. Victorian villas that either looked out to the sea or across the moor. Later larger homes had been built throughout the twentieth century and Westergate was now very much the moneyed side of Eashire. Having said that, Colm pulled up in front of a modest detached Edwardian home with a curving roof line and mock Tudor beams. Although there was a drive it was full with a BMW, with a two year old plate and a brand new Mini. Kate felt that this latest model had been injected with steroids.

Walking up the gravel drive Kate noted that the garden had been tidied for winter. Colm rapped firmly on the door using a lion headed knocker. From within they heard a female voice calling out and then the sound of heavy footsteps on wooden stairs. The door opened and a young woman, with similar fashion sense to Terry, stood. Her torn jeans fashionably tight and her jumper equally loose.

Kate held up her warrant and introduced herself and Colm. "We would like to talk with Mrs Maisie Blaiseforth-Brown."

The young woman, Kate hazarded that this was probably Clare, seemed remarkably disinterested. She called over her shoulder, "Mum. It's the police. They want to talk to you."

Kate heard the tone of exclamation but not the word. A woman came from the back of the house wiping her hands on a tea towel. "Police?"

Kate went through the introductions again. "We would like a few words, if we may Mrs Blaiseforth-Brown?" Kate said.

"Oh. Right." Good manners took over. "Of course. Do come this way. Can I get you a drink? And please call me Maisie."

They both declined the refreshment as they followed her into a sitting room. A fire was gently playing in the hearth and there was a sense of homeliness.

"Please, do sit down. Now, how may I help you?" She sat herself in one of the fireside chairs while Kate and Colm sat on the sofa facing her. Mrs Brown sat on the edge of her seat; unable to settle back with such unexpected visitors.

Kate began. "We are investigating the death of Elise Betteridge."

Maisie's brow wrinkled in confusion. "Investigating her death. I was told it was a heart attack. It wasn't?"

"A number of inconsistences came to light with the post-mortem and so we have to follow up with some questions." Kate explained.

"Oh my goodness!" Maisie covered her mouth, horror in her eyes. "You don't mean she was murdered?" She gave a nervous laugh, half expecting them to dismiss her idea. They didn't.

"We are just trying to answer some questions at this stage." Kate placated. "When was the last time you saw or spoke with Miss Betteridge?"

Maisie sat back in the chair. "I was invited to a special meeting on Monday and then Ken and I spent another forty minutes or so with Elise in her office."

"Was this to discuss her plans to include an American college in Blaiseforth's future?" Colm asked.

Maisie nodded. "Yes."

"What were your feelings about this plan?" Kate asked.

Maisie now sat up straight. "I think it's a terrible idea and I told Elise so. That was not the ethos behind my ancestors' plans for the school."

"How did she take your rejection?"

Maisie paused and thought. "I think she hoped she would win me round. She gave Ken all the educational information and he was going to report back to a trustees meeting next month. I think she hoped that he would see it as a positive and persuade the trustees of its benefits."

"What if you were still against the idea?" Colm asked.

Maisie laughed softly. "If I was outvoted it would go through. I don't have special voting or decision making rights, even if I am a Blaiseforth."

"Do you think you will be won over?" Kate

asked.

"I don't know. I don't want to appear intractable but I can't see it fulfilling the ethos my ancestors started with."

"What about when…" Colm consulted his notebook, "when Dr Wingfield introduced day girls?"

"Oh that was all in keeping with their ideals. 'Blaiseforth providing excellent educational experiences for girls in Eashire.'" Maisie sounded like she was quoting from somewhere.

Kate raised an inquiring eyebrow and Maisie explained. "It's one of the points in the original trust's constitution."

Maisie leant forward, almost conspiratorially, "If it wasn't a heart attack how did Elise die?"

"I'm afraid at this stage of our investigation we are unable to discuss the details." Kate said formally.

Maisie put her hand up and was a little breathless when she said, "Of course. Crass of me to ask."

"What did you think of Miss Betteridge?" Colm asked.

"Think of her?"

"We're trying to get a sense of the type of person she was."

"Oh, I see." She shifted in her seat a little before beginning. "She wasn't someone I warmed to. Not that she was unpleasant or dictatorial but she was very..." She paused, obviously searching for the right word. "Very focused on the school. Everything she did was about increasing the success of the school."

"Even the American college?"

Maisie made a little grimace of distaste. "Yes, even that. Elise was quite sure it was what the school needed."

"Is it usual to appoint an old girl to the teaching staff of the school?" Kate asked. "I noticed that both Miss Betteridge and Miss Sandford are former pupils."

"Not usual, as in we would always appoint an old girl but in both their cases they were the best candidates. Elise had quite a varied and, I suppose you would call it, a glittering career. After she finished her post grad teaching course she went abroad to..." she paused, "I think it was South Africa, and taught for about seven years. Her focus, even then, was on girls' education. When back in this country she had a number of posts in prestigious girls' schools, each appointment a step up and on from the one before."

Kate nodded. "Do you know if she has any family?"

"No," said Maisie. "I know her parents are dead and she was an only child. I never heard her mention any other relatives."

Colm took up the thread, "Would you say Miss Betteridge was a loner?"

Again Maisie paused, "I suppose, yes. She was very happy in her own company. Apart from Beth, Beth Sandford, I don't think she had friends within the staff. Although there is Miss Hazel at Witcham."

"Thank you. Yes we know about Miss Hazel."

"Well, if that's all..." Maisie moved as though to rise and steer her guests to the door.

"Before we go could we have a word with Clare, please? It won't take long."

"Clare?"

"Just to get a different perspective on Miss Betteridge and the school."

"Ah, yes. I'll go and find her."

CHAPTER 20

"She wasn't keen on us talking to the daughter," Colm surmised.

"No. But would any parent?"

Further conversation was forestalled by the arrival of Clare. Maisie hung in the door way, clearly not wanting to leave Clare alone with them.

"Thank you Mrs Blaiseforth-Brown." The return to the formal mode of address seemed to work and Maisie left pulling the door to as she went.

Clare launched straight in once her mother had gone. "Mum says Miss Betteridge was murdered." Anticipation hung in the air.

"No," Kate said. "There are inconsistencies about her death that we need to find the answers to."

Clare sunk back into the chair vacated by her mother, deflated. Colm turned on his charm. "We wanted a younger person's perspective on what Blaiseforth and the staff are like. You were there at the chalk face so to speak."

"We are past the chalk stage," Clare's tone was sardonic and she gave Kate an appraising look. Colm's easy charm was not going to work here.

"What did you think of Miss Betteridge? Did

you know Dr Wingfield, before her?"

"I had just started in Year 9 when Betty arrived." Unlike Izzy's dismay at letting slip the slight disrespect in the name, Clare seemed to revel in it. "In fairness she seemed all right. Very keen on all girls going on to university and having very high goals. But not really a people person. She relied on Miss Sandford for that kind of input." There was a note of respect in her voice at the mention of Beth Sandford that had certainly been missing from her talk about the dead headteacher.

"Did you respect Miss Betteridge?" Colm asked. Kate thought she knew the answer.

"Respect? May be. There was this one time that she had to teach us English lit. There was a spate of sickness and diarrhoea. I think I was in year eleven because we were reading To Kill a Mockingbird. Do you know it?"

Both Kate and Colm nodded. "Well do you remember that scene when the townsfolk come to the jail to lynch the guy Atticus is defending and it's Scout singling out some of them that stops them acting like a group and become individuals again?" Again both nodded their heads. "Well Miss Betteridge said that was one of the most powerful moments in the book and that we needed to learn to think as individuals and not become part of the crowd. It was like she had been there."

Clare shook her head. "I've not explained that

very well but it was obviously something really important to her. It's the only time I saw her show passion."

"Thank you, Clare. That really is helpful. It gives us more of an idea of the type of person she was." Colm made to get up and leave but Kate had another question.

"Clare, who do the girls go to if they want something they're not allowed? You know, ciggies, drink, perhaps even drugs?"

Clare fidgeted, clearly uncomfortable with the new direction of questioning. Kate leant forward. "This won't go any further but it's information we need." She leant back again and stared at a point above Clare's head. "I would imagine that it would need to be a day girl. You don't have to give us a name, but would I be on the right track?"

Clare nodded before adding, "When I was there it was normally one of two day girls that were asked to bring stuff in. Normally on a PE day so it wasn't obvious that they'd got extra stuff."

"Any idea if the same system is running now?"

There was a clear hesitation. Kate tried to reassure, "Your name will not be mentioned but if you know anything it would be really helpful to this investigation and clear up some of the questions we have about Miss Betteridge's death."

Whether it was the reminder about why the police were there but Clare nodded, "I'm not sure who, but there was a rumour that one of the boarders in year eight or nine, below me, could get her hands on most things. And yes, drugs were part of it. Mostly weed…" She tailed off. The implication being that it wasn't only weed.

"Any idea who?" Kate asked.

"No, it was someone who had more access to Eashire than most boarders. I really don't know any more." Clare shook her head again.

Kate wasn't inclined to believe her but let it go for the moment. "Thank you, Clare. We'll get out of your hair now." This time they both made to rise and leave.

CHAPTER 21

"Where to next, boss?"

"Where does Sir Ken Grant live in relation to where we are now?" Kate asked.

Colm peered over her shoulder at the sheet of trustees and their addresses. "That's back towards the town centre."

"Okay, let's head for there but can we stop somewhere for a coffee?"

"No problem. There's a really good café just up the road. A bit pricey but brilliant coffee."

As Colm executed a perfect three-point turn he asked, "Do you think Clare really doesn't know who the go to girl is now?"

Kate mused out loud, "I'm not sure but whoever it is she was in Year 9 three years ago so she would now be in the lower sixth. Who do we know in the lower sixth?"

Kate caught Colm's surprised glance. "You're not thinking it's one of the girls after all?"

"I really don't know but it's a connection we can't ignore," Kate sighed.

As Colm drew up outside a café that was trying to survive the weather in its pretence that Eashire could copy the French street life, Kate passed him a fiver, "Latte, full milk, two sugars. How long will it take us to get to Sir Grant's?"

Colm took the money and hazarded, "About

twenty minutes."

"I'll give him a call while you're getting the coffees."

On Colm's return, two steaming open containers of coffee in his hands, Kate pushed open the driver's door and relieved him of the cup he offered. "Due at Sir K's by midday. That gives us twenty minutes to enjoy the coffee."

Before she had finished speaking, her mobile sounded. Colm grinned at the ring tone.

"DI Medlar... Really? That was quick work, especially at a weekend. I'll take a look when I'm back in." Kate looked at Colm and smiled. "No, we're going back to the school this afternoon... If not see you Monday. Thanks Len."

Kate put her phone away and turned to Colm, "It's not often you can say you're pleased to hear from Len Goodfellow but he says forensics have some fingerprints but no matches at the moment."

Colm nodded and reflected on the news. "Find the owners, find our murderer?"

"Hard to say but access to the Head's sitting room has got to be limited, hasn't it?"

Colm nodded again and blew on his coffee. As he settled back in his seat he asked, "How come you have full fat milk *and* sugar and you're built like, what my Gran would call, a racing snake."

Kate chuckled. "Racing snake. I've not heard that one before. Genetics I'm afraid. My Dad was stick thin and could eat everyone under the table.

I think we just have faster metabolisms. If it's any consolation it doesn't make us healthier: Dad died a few years back from blocked arteries and a massive stroke. He was only fifty-nine."

"Sorry, boss."

Kate waved a hand. "No. It's okay. We didn't have a great relationship. He didn't think women should escape the kitchen. I'm afraid from my early teens onwards we fought as often as we met."

Colm seemed to nod but he could have just been bobbing his lips to the hot coffee to check its drinkability. "What about your Mum?"

"She is amazing! I realise now how much I underestimated her. When Dad was alive she was the woman in the kitchen and I thought that was the whole story but what I didn't know was that the good works she got involved with once I'd left home was much more than she let on to me. I'm not sure that Dad knew the whole of it. She used her kitchen skills to start a soup kitchen in the local church hall and now she provides meals for the homeless and the poor. She's even got into takeaways."

Colm smiled, "She sounds amazing."

Kate looked into the middle distance, "When I was last home I went to see what she did. I thought she was just the cook but she runs the whole thing and goes out to meet potential sponsors. She's got the local supermarket giving her sell by food each day which she makes into all sorts!" The pride and warmth were evident in her voice. Embarrassed to have shared so much Kate asked, "What about your parents?"

Colm smiled broadly, "Oh both very much alive. They are sheep farmers. My Mum is as much a part of the business as Dad. I know there will come a time when they're going to have to step back but my sister, also a Kate, is part of the business and she will take on more. And Andy, my younger brother, he's still in school, fifteen, I think he wants to follow in the family footsteps."

"But not you?"

"I help out on the farm when I can but no, I knew it wasn't what I wanted to do with my life," said Colm.

"So why the police?"

"I was aiming for forensics but my sciences weren't good enough and a careers advisor pointed me towards a new course that was basically a police course. We studied the law, the history of policing, modern stuff and international. That sort of thing. So I got my degree and then joined up."

Colm glanced at his watch. "Drink up. Time to make a move."

Simultaneously they drained their cups and Kate hopped out and put the cups in a bin provided by the café. Colm started the engine and they were away.

CHAPTER 22

Parking near Sir Kenneth's house was impossible and in the end Kate told Colm to park on double yellows and put a Police Officer sign in the front window. Sir Kenneth lived in the oldest part of Eashire and Kate was not surprised when the address brought them to the small, worn, oak door set into worked stone. "What age is this do you think?" Kate asked.

"The tourist people think these two streets," he pointed to the street at the end and the one they were stood in, "are the original buildings of Eashire, so at least medieval."

A large round wrought iron knocker made a sound that echoed in the street and brought its owner to the door. Sir Kenneth was a small, portly, slightly balding man in his late sixties, Kate guessed. He smiled warmly, "DCI Medlar, come in."

"It's DI Medlar sir, and this is my colleague DC Hunter."

"Well I'm sure you deserve a promotion," he chuckled good-naturedly. "Do mind your head, DC Hunter, our ancestors were not as tall as you in the main."

Colm did have to duck his head as he came in and again every time they passed under a beam. Stone walls and stone flags should have made the hall cold but it was beautifully warm. Sir Kenneth led them through to a wood panelled room. Kate thought you only normally saw such rooms in telly programmes, not real life.

A fire, literally roared in a deep hearth. "I just put on another log for you. Please sit in the chairs either side." With that he went and pulled a dark wood, heavy chair from the wall to sit between the two officers.

Having sat and got comfortable Sir Kenneth began, "You were very mysterious on the phone DI Medlar, something about poor Elise?"

"Yes, sir. Unfortunately, the pathologist found some inconsistencies with Miss Betteridge's death and does not believe that heart failure was the cause of death."

Sir Kenneth seemed to mull this over before saying matter-of-factly, "So you believe she was murdered?"

"At this stage we are unable to confirm or deny that supposition, sir, but it is a possibility."

Sir Kenneth shook in disbelief, "What on earth could Elise have done to warrant her death? I find this very hard to believe, detective."

Kate nodded. The more she found out about Elise Betteridge the less she could believe she had been deliberately murdered.

"So what do you need to know?"

"How long have you known Miss Betteridge, sir?" Colm asked.

Sir Kenneth looked up at the mantelpiece,

"Well certainly since she took over as Head at Blaiseforth but I also knew of her through my work." Seeing blank looks he explained. "I was a lecturer in Educational Science at Oxford and had seats on various working parties where I came across Elise. It was something to do with single sex education: you know the benefits for girls and boys." He paused and seemed to wander, "You know we got some very interesting results. It seems girls get far more out of single sex education than boys do."

"So did you know her socially, sir?" Colm wanted clarification on their relationship.

"No, not really. We have shared drinks in the evening of a conference, along with other delegates, but no. I don't think Elise did social interaction. She was very focused on her work. Very single minded." He seemed to want to praise Miss Betteridge's commitment.

"Were you part of the panel that appointed Miss Betteridge?" Kate asked.

Sir Kenneth nodded. "I had to declare my former acquaintanceship with her but it was seen as an advantage in the interviewing process."

"And you have worked closely with her since her appointment?" Colm asked.

"Really only in the last eighteen months, when I became the chair of the trustees, before that it was Glyn Edwards."

Kate looked down at her list of trustees

but failed to find Glyn Edwards' name. "Is Mr Edwards no longer a trustee?"

"No, poor chap. Cancer. Died just before this last Christmas."

Well that was a small mystery solved but they weren't getting anything useful here. "What about Miss Betteridge's plan to incorporate the American college?

"Ah yes. Very interesting." He leaned back and seemed to grow with pride or contentment. "I'm presenting a summary of the pros and cons to the trustees next month but so far it seems to be a very sensible idea. It will bring in more money, more pupils and give the school an international standing."

"Mrs Blaiseforth-Brown seems to feel that it will go against the original purpose of the trust and the establishment of the school?" Kate suggested.

"Um! I don't want to talk out of turn but I think Maisie's problem is about a lack of legacy." He saw Kate's blank expression, "She is worried that the Blaiseforth name will stop being an important part of Eashire's society and history."

"So her concern is more about the family name than the benefits for the school?" Colm supplied.

"Well, I don't want to cast aspersions but the fact that she insisted on becoming double barrelled rather than give up her family name must say something?"

"But, on the whole you were happy with the idea?" Kate persisted.

"I haven't finished examining all the paperwork Elise supplied but at this stage, yes, I think I can say that I would vote the proposal in."

"We understand you had further discussions with Miss Betteridge after the meeting."

"Yes. Maisie came along as well. I think Elise just wanted to make sure I had everything I needed to analyse the impact of a partnership with the American college. I couldn't stay long as I was due at my daughter's for supper and I wanted to see my grandson before he disappeared to bed."

Kate looked at Colm who closed his notebook. Kate rose and held out her hand to Sir Kenneth, "Thank you, sir. That has helped us clarify some thoughts."

If they needed to they could check his alibi for that evening but it didn't seem likely that Sir Kenneth had a motive for killing Elise Betteridge.

"My pleasure. Any time." He spoke over his shoulder as he led them back onto the street.

CHAPTER 23

Walking back to the car Kate asked, "Colm, you okay with a sandwich in the car before we go back to the school? I want to have a chat with the staff that live on the same floor as Miss Betteridge and I need to check with Miss Sandford where she was for the evening of the murder."

"You don't think she's behind it, do you, boss?"

Kate sighed deeply. "No, but I can't get a handle on anyone else either so might as well cross all the t's."

"Okay. I know where we can pick up food and a coffee."

Steaming the car windows up with their hot drinks Kate and Colm went over the main facts again but still nothing sprung out. "Bart says follow the money."

"What money?"

"That I don't know but he thinks the motive here is either passion or money and it doesn't look like Elise Betteridge was one for passion, does it?"

"Do you think she was embezzling money?" questioned Colm.

"I doubt it with the new build and American college idea. And even if she was, is it a killing issue?"

Colm shook his head. "And that's a problem isn't it? No-one has any kind of motive. We must be missing something."

Kate agreed, but what?

Lunch over, Colm drove them back to the school. As they turned in the drive they followed a coach bearing the logo of another school, not one either of them knew.

"Match day." Colm said knowledgeably.

"Which hopefully means the staff members we need to talk to will be free." Then Kate had an idea. "Tell you what. You go and be your charming self on the touch line and see if you can find out anything. Attitudes to our victim, home or away. Any gossip. You know the sort of thing."

Colm nodded and once out of the car followed the disappearing coach round to the side of the school. Kate made her way up the main steps again. The foyer was deserted and the reception office locked. Out of politeness Kate knocked at the Head's office as well. Just to let Beth Sandford know she was around but that too was locked. Kate shrugged. Well, she'd tried.

Kate knocked on the first door on her left, consulting her notebook she found this should be Dr Heath. She waited a few minutes before she heard hesitant footsteps on the other side of the door. When opened a small lady, leaning heavily on a cane stood in the doorway. "Ah, DI Medlar, I believe?"

"Yes. Dr Heath?" Kate guessed Dr Heath must be in the retirement bracket. Mid to late sixties, she thought.

"Indeed. Come in. Can I get you anything to eat or drink? Have you lunched?

Kate nodded. "I'm fine, thank you."

The room was a smaller and less sunlit version of Miss Betteridge's sitting room. The main thing was the lack of a bay window and so one side of the room was taken up with a large desk and book shelves and then two comfortable chairs around a hearth. A mock coal fire was lit, giving the room a cosy feel. A gentle scent of rose was in the air; delicate but recognisable.

"If you would like to take the left-hand chair," Dr Heath pointed, "The right-hand one has worn to my shape!" She laughed.

Kate could see a keen intelligence as Dr Heath regarded her across the multi-coloured rug. "Beth has spoken with all of us, the staff that is, and we know that you are regarding Elise's death as suspicious. I have to tell you that I find that incredibly hard to believe. Elise was not someone who evoked great passions in other people and surely there must be passion behind murder?"

"Not necessarily, but yes normally there is a clear motive and we have been unable to establish what that could be."

Dr Heath nodded. "Well I am sure you have your reasons for thinking it was not a heart attack. Now what would you like to ask?"

"On the evening of Miss Betteridge's death were you in here?"

"Yes. I came up about six-thirty, after the girls had their supper. There was marking for the upper sixth to complete for the following day and tidying up my lesson plans for the day after."

"So you were here until what time?"

"I retired to bed about ten, read for a while and put my light out at ten forty-five. I like to listen to Radio 4's bedtime story."

"At any point in the evening did you go out onto the landing or hear anything unusual from Miss Betteridge's room?"

"I am sorry, my dear. Nothing. I didn't even hear the supper girl and I sometimes do."

"Miss Sandford said that you often have a light supper rather than a main meal of an evening. Did you do that on Monday?"

Dr Heath nodded. "I had a quick cuppa and a slice of toast about five fifteen before I went to dinner duty."

"And was the kitchenette as you would expect to find it?"

Dr Heath looked puzzled. "Well, yes. I didn't notice anything out of the ordinary."

Having nothing more to ask about the night of the murder Kate tried to elicit some more background about Miss Betteridge. "You said that Elise was unlikely to arouse strong passions. Would you say she was a cold person?"

Dr Heath looked into the flames before

turning her gaze back to Kate, "Cold? No. She was very single minded. This school. Girls' education. Those were the driving forces in her life. Her relationship with most staff was friendly but distant."

Kate caught the 'most staff' and enquired about who was not part of that group.

"I think she found some of the younger staff were lacking..." she paused, "I think the word may be dedication. Those of us who are in our late fifties and sixties knew that teaching in a girls' private school meant a certain type of lifestyle. Nowadays the younger staff tend to live off site and the school is not always their priority."

Kate thought she understood, "Was there anyone in particular whom she was not so sure of?"

"The only one that I felt, and please understand this is just my interpretation, I have no facts or proof, but I felt she found Ms Fleet a little wearing."

"Was this to do with Catherine Stanton?"

"Ah, you know about that. I think that was part of it but I think she also thought that Ms Fleet was too... open about her own sexuality." Dr Heath gave Kate a knowing look. Kate nodded her understanding.

With nothing more to add, Kate thanked Dr Heath and took her leave.

CHAPTER 24

Miss Clements turned out to be Miss Clemont, with a silent 't'. Kate assumed she must have misheard Beth Sandford earlier. Miss Clemont was an unusual find. Kate guessed her age to be late twenties, early thirties at a real push. Her youthful enthusiasm seemed out of place in the little sitting room, which was a mirror image of Dr Heath's room, even down to the two comfortable chairs. Kate thought she had an elegance about her. Was that a bit stereotypical? She's French so she must be elegant? Kate wondered why Miss Clemont was occupying one of these suites of rooms as she had been led to believe that they were for senior staff. As though guessing Kate's train of thought Miss Clemont explained, "Miss Betteridge, she allows me to live here because I cannot drive and could not find rooms close by. I am here on exchange for one year."

Kate nodded, "So your counterpart is in France teaching English?"

"Oui, Miss Barraclough. We change back in the summer."

"So Miss Betteridge was very kind to you. Did you like her?"

Miss Clemont frowned very daintily, "She was very..." she seemed to be searching for the words, "how you say? Professional. Not a warm person but good at being a headteacher."

"On the night of her death were you here all evening?"

"Mais Non! I am helping in Woolf house until lights out at ten o' clock," said Miss Clemont.

"And you didn't notice anything when you returned here?"

"Non. Everything is quiet." She gave a very Gallic shrug.

"How do you like it here? Is it very different from France?"

"It is different. The girls here they think learning another language is…" she stumbled for the words, "I think, not needed. 'Everyone learns English'." She made quotation marks in the air. "In France we think it is good to learn other languages."

"So no budding linguists amongst them?"

"Oh no. You misunderstand. That is the attitude of most girls but there are some very good linguists here. I am hoping that Kitty Hardcastle will win the Blaiseforth prize this year. She has already higher certificates in French and German and now she is studying Latin, Spanish and Mandarin!"

"Wow. That is amazing. Do you teach all those subjects?"

"Non. French, German, Spanish and English I speak. Kitty has two special tutors for the Latin and Mandarin."

"Mandarin must be very hard to learn, with it being a different alphabet as well."

"Most definitely," agreed Miss Clemont, "but she is, what you call, gifted. Learning a new language for her is like a bird to water."

Kate smiled. "The saying is 'duck to water', specifically rather than just bird."

"Thank you. I find your idioms very confusing. Can you tell me why it is always 'raining cats and dogs'?"

Kate laughed. "I really have no idea. It's just one of those things we say. I suppose it's a cultural thing, everyone knows you mean it is very wet when you say it."

Miss Clemont nodded. "We have similar saying in French. When I translate them into English they make no sense."

Kate got the conversation back onto a track she wanted to explore. "You mentioned the Blaiseforth prize. What is that?"

"I do not know the details but an outstanding pupil in the lower sixth may enter for the prize. It is money to help with further education. Miss Sandford would know more."

Kate thought it strange that the school had such a prize. Surely if the girls' parents could afford to pay the school fees they could also afford the costs of university. She would need to check the details. "Is Kitty the only entrant this year?"

"I believe that Isabelle Grey has entered and maybe one other, but I do not know who or why."

"Thank you, Miss Clemont. I hope you continue to enjoy your time here. I wish I spoke French as well as you speak English. I only have school girl French and I haven't used that for years."

"You must practice. You will be surprised at how much will return."

"Thank you." Kate rose, as did Miss Clemont. As Kate was opening the door Miss Clemont said, "It is sad. Miss Betteridge. I think you will find the person?"

"I certainly intend to," Kate confirmed as she left.

CHAPTER 25

The final teacher to interview today was Miss Hooper. A middle aged woman opened the door sharply. She was dressed in dust covered dungarees and a shabby jumper, underneath the braces. Her hair was short and held back from her face with a scarf. To Kate she looked like something out of the 1950s.

"Ah. DI Medlar. I was beginning to think Beth had got it wrong."

Kate was a little taken aback and it must have shown because Miss Hooper held out a hand, as if in appeasement, "Sorry, that was very rude of me, it's just that I have a project on the go and Saturday afternoon is my best time to get things done."

"Project?" Kate queried.

"Yes. I am an artist. Not that I can make it pay, which is why I double as an art teacher here, but it does mean I have access to a workshop and the kiln."

"Do you make pots?" Kate floundered.

"No. I'm into sculpture," as though seeing Kate conjuring up Michelangelo's David she continued, "They are for the discerning home." There was a self-deprecating, even mocking note in her voice.

"Right." Kate wasn't sure what else to say and

Miss Hooper seemed to take pity on her.

"Come on in. Pull up a chair, there might be one not covered in stone dust... You want to ask me about Elise?"

"Yes. How did you find her?"

"She was determined and single-minded in her dedication to the school and education but she also had a soul."

Kate was surprised. "Soul?"

"She would come to my workshop and sit and watch me working. I think she found it therapeutic and she understood what I was trying to achieve. We never spoke about it outside my workshop, not even when we'd meet by accident on the landing here."

"I get the impression that she was a little distant with everyone. Would you agree?"

"Yes, in part." There was a pause, "As I say, something about my art captivated her but I also think that in these last few months something had pierced her armour."

"What? A good or bad thing? How was she different for you to notice this change?"

Miss Hooper leaned back and thought, "It was a good thing, I am sure. She seemed softer, somehow." She paused and blew her cheeks out, "I'm not really sure how she was different but I think she was."

"What about the evening of her death, did you hear or see anything?"

"I was in my workshop until about seven-thirty and took a shower immediately I got back." She paused, "I may have heard the supper tray being collected but I can't be sure. It's a sound you become accustomed to and I can't be sure that I heard it on that night or I just think I remember hearing it."

Kate nodded her understanding. "I was just speaking with Miss Clemont and she talked about the Blaiseforth Prize but seemed unsure of the details."

Miss Hooper frowned, probably at the non sequitur nature of the question but she answered. "I'm not sure when it started but it is a monetary prize for an outstanding scholar."

Kate voiced the thought she'd had when speaking to Miss Clemont. "It seems strange to have such a thing in a school like Blaiseforth. Surely if the parents can afford the school fees they can afford the next stage of their daughter's education?"

Miss Hooper nodded in understanding but explained, "The prize offers the girl a chance for extras. If an artist won it she could use the prize to visit galleries throughout the world. And you may be surprised to know that a large number of our parents scrimp and save to put their daughter through here and they don't always have the extra resources needed for university."

Kate nodded. "So can anyone be considered for the prize?"

"Well she has to show that she has a genuine

talent for a subject and she needs to have the written support of at least two of her teachers. This all happens in the lower sixth. So we have a contest on at the moment."

"Oh really. Who decides the winner and when is it announced?"

"It is normally a team of house mistresses, Miss Sandford and the Head. Then the winner is announced as part of our prize giving assembly in the last week of June.

"So quite a wait for the girls concerned? Do you have many who enter?"

"It tends to be two or three each year, because they need the teachers' support."

Trying to make it sound like a casual question Kate asked, "So who's in the running this year?"

Miss Hooper rubbed her forehead, "I know it's no-one from the arts side of the school. I believe Kitty Hardcastle has entered. She is an amazing linguist and took some of her A-levels two years early. Then of course there's the IT guru," she smiled fondly, "Izzy Grey is the go to girl if you have any IT problems. An absolute marvel. I think Chloe Millar may be another contender, she is superb at the sciences."

Kate smiled, "Who's your money on?"

"I've no idea. And every year I am grateful that I'm not on the panel that has to decide." Clearly feeling that Kate had consumed enough of her time Miss Hooper rose to indicate she needed to be going back to her project. Kate took the hint and thanked Miss Hooper for her time.

As she was leaving Miss Hooper said, "She was a good woman and I think Blaiseforth has lost one of its greatest assets."

"Thank you." Kate thought about her words as she walked down the stairs. Miss Hooper's words were probably the most affectionate she had heard so far about Elise Betteridge.

CHAPTER 26

Feeling no further forward and, in truth, a little dejected Kate stepped outside to find Colm. The winter made dusk early and already the light was fading. Kate followed the sound of cheering voices and the glow of pitch lights and found the last match of the afternoon drawing to a close. Colm was not hard to spot as there were very few men present in the crowd.

A group of girls in Blaiseforth colours lined one end and were shouting their encouragement to the team on the field. A roar went up as Blaiseforth took possession of the ball. "Shoot! Shoot!" echoed across the pitch. There was a miniscule pause and then screams of delight as Blaiseforth scored and the final whistle blew.

Colm had spotted her and raised an arm in acknowledgement. While girls streamed onto the field he made his way across to where Kate stood. "I didn't know lacrosse could be so exciting," he smiled. "You should have seen the goal keeper. Fearless. You wouldn't get me on the pitch with them without full armour."

"Pick up anything interesting?"

Colm rubbed his chin and Kate heard the whisper of stubble being smoothed. "Bits and pieces." He drew his brows together. "Everyone seems to feel Miss Betteridge was an okay Head -

staff and pupils. I did find out a little more about Kitty Hardcastle and Izzy Grey." He turned to head back to the car.

"Kitty is a genius but doesn't cope well with the real world so losing her text is typical. The other girls in her year try to look out for her but she is prone to losing things and minor accidents."

"What kind of accidents?"

"Apparently some of the girls have riding lessons, Kitty amongst them and a few months ago she forgot to buckle the girth strap. Well no, that's not strictly true. She must have partially buckled up but not made sure it was secure. The saddle was fine whilst they were walking to the tracks but once she started into a trot and then canter the whole thing just turned like a key in a lock. She had a very nasty fall. Fortunately, they were on grass and she was wearing a hat, otherwise it could have been a lot worse."

"Anything else?"

"Um, there was something about her falling down the stairs in her house at the school just before Christmas. She was convinced she'd tripped on something but nothing was found."

"Any chance these could be more than accidents?" Kate mused.

Colm rubbed his chin again. "No-one seems to think so. What are you thinking?"

Kate signed. "No, nothing. Just trying to find something. Anything to hook this murder on."

"Anything about Izzy Grey?"

"Well liked by most. Runs the computer club at the school and is always approachable when younger girls have IT problems. I did get the impression, however, from a few in her own year group that there was something else but no-one was letting it slip."

"Do you think she could be the fixer?"

"I suppose it's possible."

"We need to continue our chat with Mrs Jessop and find out how Izzy spends her holidays. I am sure she can't be tied to the school the entire time. Perhaps she has made contact with some of the youths from the Camworth Estate."

Colm raise a quizzical eyebrow. "Seems a bit of a long shot, boss."

"Do you have any better ideas?" Kate snapped.

Colm raised his hands in submission and Kate ran hers through her hair giving it a decided punk flavour. "Sorry Colm. I'll drive back to town. Where do you want dropping off?"

Colm gave directions and Kate dropped him less than twenty minutes later. The conversation had been a little stilted.

"I'll see you at the station Monday morning and then we're back to the school. I want another chat with Beth Sandford – we haven't actually asked what she was doing Monday evening and we need to follow up on Ms Fleet and Mrs Chapman."

"Okay, boss. See you Monday."

Kate watched in her rear view mirror as Colm strode away, disappearing into the last of the shoppers on Eashire's high street. Kate debated about checking into the station to look at the forensic results but fingerprints could only help if you had a suspect. In the end she headed home.

Transcript Audio Log 23 secs

The police were in in force today. Most of the staff seem to have been interviewed in the meeting room this morning and I noticed the man and woman back again this afternoon. I don't know what she was doing but he came and watched us play. Not many schools have lacrosse teams so it was good to be on the pitch today. I find the imminent danger vitalising. And made some brilliant saves and we won, thanks to me. I wonder what the woman was up to.

CHAPTER 27

Kate found that her usual routine of a cup of tea and a slice of toast in bed with The Archers was not having its normal soothing effect. If her mind wasn't running in diminishing circles about the case it was off over thinking Robin's upcoming meeting. Finally, with much huffing and puffing she threw the duvet back and headed for the shower hoping that a beating from the hot water would drive a better mood into her head.

Refreshed but no further forward she decided that she would carry on interviewing people today. Bugger it! Even if it was a Sunday. She would go and visit Miss Hazel. The only person that Elise Betteridge seemed to have a social connection with. Kate opened her laptop and found the address and tapped it into her phone for the Satnav.

Despite being mid-February it was a pleasant day. It had obviously been very cold overnight but the morning sunshine had enough heat behind it to actually clear her car. As she drove she thought some of the trees were gaining that slightly fuzzy look that hinted at buds waiting to burst forth. She really should appreciate this more, she thought. Kate had not been so aware of the seasons working in the city. There it was either a warm day or a cold day. Wet or dry. The sense of seasons was totally missing.

The drive to Witcham was pleasant. It was still a village in its own right, although the houses from Eashire were putting out tentacles along the main route in. Give it another twenty years, Kate thought and Witcham would be just another area within Eashire. The Orchard was a newly built residential care place. Landscaped gardens contained numerous paths offering routes through and round it as well as regular benches for those who wished or needed to sit for a while.

Kate parked her car and entered through an automatic door. Ahead of her was an unstaffed desk and several corridors off. Directly in front was a large sitting room with a conservatory and the February sun shone brightly down. Kate looked at the photographs of the staff displayed on one of the two noticeboards. Apart from the handyman everyone else was a woman, even the gardener. She wondered if the male residents minded seeing so few able bodied men around the place.

Her thoughts were interrupted by a bright and breezy voice coming from behind. Kate turned and recognised one of the faces from the board but couldn't remember the name. "Good afternoon, how may I help you?" the woman asked.

Kate showed her warrant card and asked, "Is

it possible to talk to Miss Hazel, please?"

The woman's eyebrows disappeared into her fringe, "Miss Hazel? Are you sure you have the right name?"

"Quite sure, thank you. Do you know Miss Betteridge? I believe she visits Miss Hazel each week."

"Miss Betteridge, of course but she hasn't been to see Miss Hazel for a few weeks. She was regular as clockwork, Sunday afternoon, two to four o'clock for years and then a few months ago her visits were more, random. Still Sundays but sometimes in the morning, sometimes later in the early evening and quite a few no shows."

Interesting thought Kate. Where was Miss Betteridge going? Or was she just too busy at the school? Mrs Jessop gave the impression that it was still an ongoing occurrence. "Do you know and does Miss Hazel know that Miss Betteridge died last week?"

The woman's eyebrows disappeared again. "Died? Oh no. Poor Miss Hazel, she'll be devastated. They've known each other for about fifty years I think she said, once."

"So would you direct me to her, please?"

"She'll be in her room, number eighteen. She doesn't like the television always being on in the lounge. Just follow that corridor," the woman pointed to the right. "It's on the left."

Kate made to follow the directions but

the woman called, "Would you mind signing the register of visitors, please? Fire regs!" she laughed awkwardly.

Kate stopped and signed and then followed the corridor.

CHAPTER 28

The door to room eighteen was partially open and Kate peered in before announcing herself. The room was light and warmly decorated. Miss Hazel was a small woman, a blanket around her knees and a thick cardigan buttoned up to the top. She sat in a chair like those Kate had seen advertised, that help you stand up. At the moment a bed tray was across her front and she was reading a book with a large magnifying glass.

Kate knocked on the door. Miss Hazel looked up. Kate was surprised at the enormity of eyes behind very thick lenses. "Ah, fresh meat!" Miss Hazel chuckled.

"Miss Hazel? I'm DI Medlar from Eashire CID." Kate held out her warrant card but Miss Hazel dismissed it with a wave of her hand.

"Come in dear and take a seat." She pointed to a chair opposite. "Now what could I have possibly done that needs a detective inspector to come and see me?" Kate was aware of a bright, intelligent face.

"These damn things are no good for conversation." When she removed her glasses she had lively hazel coloured eyes. Kate wondered if that was where her name had originated.

"I'm afraid I am the bearer of bad news," Kate began.

Miss Hazel sat very still. Her body tensed for a blow.

"I regret to inform you that Elise Betteridge died last Tuesday evening."

Miss Hazel seemed to implode and collapse in on herself. Her hand trembled as she reached for a paper hanky and tears silently rolled down her cheeks. Kate knew there was nothing she could do or say until Miss Hazel had absorbed that knock-out blow. She looked out of the window and thought it probably had a lovely view when the flowers were in bloom. She also thought about the fact that this was the first person she'd seen shed a tear for the victim.

After a few minutes Miss Hazel wiped her eyes, blew her nose and sat up straighter. She looked directly into Kate's eyes. "I'm assuming your presence means it was not a straight forward death?"

She certainly was still sharp. "Unfortunately, the post-mortem revealed some inconsistencies that we have to clear up. The reason for my visit is to try and gather some personal information about Miss Betteridge. Everyone I have spoken to so far merely reveal a very dedicated, single-minded woman."

Miss Hazel nodded, "That was certainly a part of her character, a big part but there was much more to Elise than that. I taught her you know?"

This time it was Kate's turn to nod. "Was she a good pupil?"

"Very. From early on it was clear that she knew what she wanted, what she needed to do to get there and set about doing it. I think this made some think that she was distant, perhaps even cold but she wasn't. She had a good sense of humour and loved folk music. During the vacations she would go to folk festivals."

Kate found it hard to equate this folk festival Elise Betteridge with the one she had created in her mind.

Miss Hazel must have seen her look of disbelief, "I know." She smiled. "She kept a lot of herself locked down. Afraid of being side tracked, I have always thought."

"I understand from the reception staff that Miss Betteridge has not been so frequent with her visits for the last few months, do you know why that was so?"

Again Miss Hazel smiled. "I think she had found love."

Kate's head spun. Of all the things she had expected as a response this was not the one she had even got on the list. "Love?" she barely managed to croak.

"Yes. It happened here. I watched it flourish."

"Here? You mean one of the residents?"

"No! Jack Newton. His wife is here in the dementia section. He comes every day, well came every day, even though she doesn't know him or anyone else from the family. In fact one afternoon her grand-daughter turned up and Audrey began to scream blue murder. I understand she even tried to get out of bed, even though she's been bed bound for months. Apparently, she seemed really afraid of her. I thank my lucky stars that my mind is still my own."

Kate murmured an agreement hoping that Miss Hazel would get to the main points. Whether she sensed this or not Miss Hazel explained. "When Elise came in the afternoon we would go to a little café they have built in the grounds. It's part of the complex but you feel like you're going out. One day, it was quiet, we were the only ones in there when Jack came in. He looked upset." She stopped, reliving the memory. "Being the nosy neighbour that I am I asked him to join us and tell us what the matter was. It transpired that his wife, Audrey, had thrown a book at him and screamed at him to go away. He was clearly very shaken by the ordeal. And that's how it started."

"What exactly started?" Kate queried.

"Elise and Jack's relationship. At first it was a cuppa in the café with me but I could see that there was a spark between them so I began to cry off. So just the two of them met and then one Sunday Elise popped in and asked would I mind if she didn't visit me but went out with Jack. I was delighted."

"So how long had this been going on?"

"Well, it was mid-summer when we had the first meeting, so six, seven months."

"Have you any idea how I can get in touch with Jack?"

"Well, if he's not in today visiting, and I think he's not because he would have made a point of telling me about Elise, then I am sure the reception can provide you with his home address."

"Thank you Miss Hazel, you have given me much more of an idea of who Elise Betteridge was. I felt that there had to be more than the two-dimensional character her staff relayed."

"Be gentle with Jack. I know he has nothing to do with Elise's death and now he will have lost two women he loved."

Kate nodded. "I will be gentle, I promise." But she was not so sure that Jack Newton wasn't a suspect. What had Bart said? Passion or money.

CHAPTER 29

Using the car's sat nav Kate found Jack Newton's house without a problem. It was on a newish housing estate with identical front gardens laid to open plan lawns and garage drives. Kate parked a little back from number thirty-two. It looked like all the others. Perhaps the lawn was a little neater, the drive had a freshly swept look, no errant leaves blowing about. She debated with herself about going to interview Jack Newton alone. He was a suspect. True, with little evidence but his surmised affair with the victim. Should she let someone know where she was going? Just in case?

She rang Colm and hoped he wasn't in the middle of something on a Sunday afternoon. His phone rang out and Kate was about to ring off when his cheerful voice came on the line, "Hi, boss. What's up?"

Kate could hear laughter and the clink of crockery in the background, "Sorry, Colm, have I called at a bad time?"

"No, boss. Perfect timing, you've got me out of clearing the table." More laughter and some cat calls greeted his words. "I came home for Sunday lunch with the family and we were just debating who was going to do what but of course work comes first!"

Kate could hear his tongue firmly in his cheek. Briefly she explained where she spent her time and the information Miss Hazel had given.

"Do you think she is on the money? You know, ninety something."

Kate laughed, "She was on the ball. I hope I'm half that fly if I get to her age."

"Okay, so now what are you up to?"

"I thought I'd go and chat with Jack Newton."

Silence on the other end. Then, "Is that a good idea?" Kate felt a spurt of irrational anger, "I think so. But if you don't hear from me in the next hour I'm at thirty-two St Catherine Close."

"Okay boss," Kate could hear the back pedalling.

"And that will leave you time to help with the washing up," Kate tried to sound light-hearted after her curtness.

Kate climbed out of her car and walked up the drive. No sign of a car but it could be in the garage. Kate rang the doorbell. In the distance she heard a pleasant chime but to her it felt like it rang on emptiness. She was proved right when a second ring still brought no-one to the door. She stepped onto the narrow patio below the sitting room window and peered in. Just a normal, clean and tidy room.

"Excuse me."

Kate turned at the voice hailing her. A youngish woman of about thirty was stood at the foot of the drive, clutching her mobile phone.

She asked, "Can I help you?" Kate took out her warrant card, "DI Kate Medlar and you are?"

"Oh, sorry. I'm Jodie Prince, number twenty-nine."

"I was after a Mr Jack Newton. He does live here?"

"Oh yes but he's away at his daughter's. I think he's a bit down about the state his wife is in and felt the need to get away."

Kate acted ignorant, "His wife?"

"Yes, Audrey, she's at The Orchard in their dementia unit." She lowered her voice as though conveying secret information, "I understand she doesn't know Jack any more. Poor man. It must be terrible. Someone you've lived with for fifty years and she doesn't know him."

Kate nodded as though in agreement with such a parlous situation but asked, "Do you know when Mr Newton is due back?"

"Tomorrow, I think," she waved her mobile around, "I could call him and check?"

"That would be very helpful but could I speak with Mr Newton, please?"

Jodie Prince dialled the number and passed her mobile to Kate. Kate heard it ringing and was at the point of thinking he wasn't going to answer when a voice asked, "Jodie? Is anything the matter?"

"Good afternoon Mr Newton. This is Detective Inspector Kate Medlar, Ms Prince kindly let me use her phone."

"Hello Inspector," he sounded confused, "is there anything I can help you with?"

"I'd like to ask you some questions about Elise Betteridge but it can wait until your return. Ms Prince suggested you would be back tomorrow, is that right?"

"Err, yes. By teatime. I'd like to go and see my wife in the evening so could we make it Tuesday morning?"

"Yes of course sir, about ten o'clock?"

"That's fine. Can I ask why you want to talk about Elise? I do know she's dead."

"Yes sir, I will explain when I see you on Tuesday."

"All right, Inspector." Kate thought he sounded weary but not wary. Only Tuesday's interview would tell.

Thanking Jodie Prince for the use of her mobile, getting Jack Newton's number and Jodie's diligence on checking up on a stranger in the close Kate left for home. It was only as she was drawing up outside her flat that she remembered she had not got back in touch with Colm. She rang him.

"How did it go, boss?"

"He wasn't in but a Neighbourhood Watch body put me in touch with him. He's away at his daughter's and will be back tomorrow evening so we have an appointment on Tuesday morning."

"Okay then. See you at the station tomorrow?"

"Yes, what about the washing up?"

Colm laughed, "My mother informed me that she would only trust me with the drying up!"

Kate laughed, "See you tomorrow, Colm."

CHAPTER 30

The following morning Kate touched base with her team. The forensic report was thorough but apart from the one set of fingerprints – middle and ring finger – everything else was smears. The prints had been found on the back of the desk chair at head height. A few fibres had been found but identified as being from polish wipes. Not a great deal to work with.

The victim's laptop and mobile were equally unremarkable. There were only two regular numbers she called, both had been identified; Jack Newton and The Orchards. Jack Newton had texted Monday evening about nine-thirty and rung but left no message about half-an-hour later. Nothing in their exchanged texts indicated anything other than good friends.

Feeling despondent, Kate turned to the financial records Alice had compiled for all the names Kate had given her. Unfortunately, the result was a big fat zero. No-one was particularly in debt, although the Chapmans sailed close to the wind at the end of each month; no-one had a mysterious past; no-one had unexplained deposits of money.

Kate scratched her head. What else? Alice watched and waited. Finally Kate said, "Would you do the same thing for Kitty, I'm assuming that's Katherine, Hardcastle and her family and for Isabelle Grey. Both in the lower sixth so you can get their approximate dates of birth."

"Anything in particular you're looking for, ma'am?"

"No. Anything that seems out of the ordinary; anything that doesn't quite make sense. You know the sort of thing, Alice"

Alice nodded. Kate left her tapping into her computer. Just as she was leaving her desk phone rang. "DI Medlar... Hello Mike... Yes, thank you for prioritising this. No! Really? How expensive?" Kate tapped a pen she had unconsciously picked up. "I'm assuming that's expensive, too? Okay. You sure? Thanks Mike. Oh, before you go, any joy on the CCTV footage? Okay thanks."

Kate put the receiver back and grinned at Colm. "I don't know if Bart will fund it but Mike says there are a couple of techniques that have just come in: one that will allow him to find out how recently the fingerprints were deposited and two, try and get DNA from the fingerprint."

"Wow! We are in the twenty-first century," Colm said with a note of admiration. Then a frown of worry appeared, "Won't they be really expensive?"

"Yes, but Mike is going to talk with Bart in terms of professional development and how infrequently we get murder cases. Not sure if it will fly but he's happy to have a go."

"What about the footage? Anything?"

"Not yet. Mike said they'd put a rush on the physical stuff but he's got someone on the cameras now."

Kate mused a few moments longer and then said, "Right, Alice you've got research. Where is Len?"

Alice shrugged.

"When he's back in he can run records for Jack Newton."

Alice nodded and Kate headed for the door with Colm in tow. Before she left she turned back, "And Alice."

"Yes, ma'am?"

"Len is to do the work."

Alice smiled grimly, "Yes, ma'am."

CHAPTER 31

Soon Kate and Colm were on the road, back to Blaiseforth Manor. Kate had brought Bart up-to-date and she felt his disappointment in their lack of progress deeply.

"You never know, Kate, perhaps this Jack Newton is your killer."

Kate had nodded but didn't have the heart to tell Bart that her instinct was that Jack Newton was just another victim in this.

Kate was reading through the interviews for Ms Fleet and Mr and Mrs Chapman. Not a lot there. Apparently Mrs Chapman had made no secret of her argument with the victim but made it sound like they were the aggrieved party. No particular sorrow from any of them about the death of the Head.

Trying to enthuse both herself and Colm she said, "Right, plan of action. I'd like you to charm Mrs Jessop and see if you can find out what it is Izzy Grey does when she 'helps'," the quote marks were evident in her tone. "I also want you to find the matron, or whatever they call the medical personnel these days, and find out what illnesses or accidents Kitty Hardcastle has experienced in the last year."

Colm looked seriously perplexed, "What do you think the connection is to our case, boss?"

Kate sighed, "I don't know but something is making me question the role of Izzy and Kitty in all this."

Colm made no reply.

Kate felt he was deliberately keeping his expression neutral. "I could be completely wide of the mark but, at the moment, apart from talking with Ms Fleet, Mrs Chapman and Jack Newton, we're getting nowhere fast."

At the school they both headed for Mrs Jessop's office. Her expression was as anxious and harried as on their first visit. "Oh, good morning Inspector, Constable. Do you still need to use the meeting room?"

"Yes, please, if that's convenient," Kate replied.

Mrs Jessop nodded her head and Kate continued, "Where will I find Ms Fleet at the moment, please?"

Mrs Jessop twirled her chair and looked at the enormous timetable behind her. With one finger she traced across it before turning back. "If you wait five minutes she will have a free lesson. Shall I find a girl to fetch her?"

"No, I don't want to put you to anymore trouble, thank you. Tell me where her room is and I'll go and find her."

"Take the left hand corridor to the stairs. Up to the first floor and right. Her room is 107."

"Thank you." Kate left, giving Colm an imperceptible nod. As she closed the door she heard Colm begin his charm offensive, "I'm so sorry we have to bother you again. I know this must be a busy time for..." Kate smiled.

While waiting for the bell Kate looked at the Blaiseforth Prize honours board. If this was all the winners it had not begun until 1928. There were a few blanks. Did that mean the prize had not been awarded? And apart from in 1983 there was just a single name for each year. 1983 had the novelty of two names. She'd ask Beth Sandford about that. Could the prize be divided?

Silence had settled on the corridor as Kate made her way to the stairs. From within each classroom there was the murmur of voices. From the cadences Kate assumed the registers were being taken. The staircase was a beautiful example of carved wood. Even the steps had small devices carved into the edges. Once upon a time the carving may have crossed the step but now the middle of each step was worn to a dusty grey.

At the first landing she turned right. These classrooms were empty but Kate could hear voices. She quietly made her way along to room 107. It was from there the voices came. An unknown female was saying, "...it's the truth. You can't keep lying to the police."

"I haven't lied, they just haven't asked." Kate recognised Beth Sandford's tones.

"They haven't asked 'yet'!" Considerable emphasis on the last word. "What will you say when they do ask?"

"I shall tell them I was in my room. Which is the truth."

"But it doesn't give you an alibi."

"For goodness sake, Jackie. You've been watching too many of those pot boiler detective shows. Why should I need an alibi? I didn't kill Elise."

"I know that! But we can account for one another, can't we. Please Beth."

"I don't see why our personal situation needs to become public knowledge."

Kate decided to make her presence known. She stepped back to the landing and then called out, "Ms Fleet?" as she walked along the corridor.

Beth Sandford looked out, "Ah, Detective Inspector Medlar. I hadn't realised you were back in."

"Only just arrived," Kate assured her. "I am looking for Ms Fleet. Is she here?"

"I'm here."

A young woman, may be thirty or more years Beth Sandford's junior, stepped past and into the corridor. She wore auburn hair, similar in colour to Kate's own, in a French plait. Her clothes were expensive and she wore them with style. A touch of make-up accentuated her eyes and the height of her cheek bones.

"How may I help you?"

"Ms Fleet would you mind coming down to the meeting room for a chat?"

Fully composed, she answered, "Yes of course. You do know that I gave a statement to one of your officers on Sunday, yesterday?"

Kate nodded. "Yes, I just have some follow up questions for you in the light of our investigation.

Ms Fleet seemed to take that in her stride. "Let me just grab my bag and I'll be with you." She disappeared back into the room.

Beth Sandford continued to hover in the doorway. Kate was sure she wanted to know how much Kate had overheard. Well she would find out later.

"Miss Sandford, could you also spare me some time later this morning? Just for some follow up questions."

She looked surprised but agreed, "I am free until lunchtime at twelve thirty-five. I will be working in Elise's, or my, office, when you are ready." With that she passed Kate and headed on down ahead of Kate and Ms Fleet.

CHAPTER 32

Ms Fleet sat and looked expectant but relaxed. Kate made a show of reading through the statement the officer had taken the previous day. She then looked up. Ms Fleet was looking out of the window, unperturbed by Kate's attempt to unsettle her. "Ms Fleet."

"Oh please call me Jackie. I toyed with the idea of getting rid of my patronym but thought that would be just too difficult in teaching and perhaps a step too far in a place like this." She indicated the building around her.

"Jackie then, what would you say your relationship was like with Miss Betteridge? Did you get on well?"

"I didn't have a great deal to do with her, really. She seemed a fair enough Head. She's only the third one I've had experience of. I can't say there was anything else."

"If you don't mind me saying, you seem to be very young to be a Head of department in a school such as Blaiseforth."

Jackie Fleet laughed, "Well thank you for the compliment." There was an underlying element of flirtation as she fluttered her lashes. She then sat up straighter, "I am young but Miss Betteridge was trying very hard to rejuvenate the staff here." Conspiratorially she added, "Have you seen the staff here? I worked out that the average age is in the region of fifty something."

"How do the other staff view you, in terms of age and experience versus youth and, what? Energy?"

"Oh they're fine. Well most of them are now. The first year was a little sticky but when they saw I could do the job and bring in some innovations without sinking the boat," she gave a coquettish grin, "even if I did rock it from time to time, they are fine."

"I understood that you had been campaigning to have the name of Catherine Stanton reinstated on the honours board in the foyer."

"Absolutely! She's an amazing writer and we shouldn't allow the mores of the past influence us now. We should be proud of her."

"And what was Miss Betteridge's view?"

"She was digging her heels in a bit but I think that was all about not allowing the new girl to be seen to have too much sway. I am sure she would have come round."

Now, Kate thought, the million dollar question, "Can you tell me where you were on the evening Miss Betteridge died. I understand you don't live in?"

"No, I don't." For the first time Kate saw a few cracks appear in the carefree façade. Kate could see the calculations going on behind Jackie's eyes. Finally, Jackie leant forward, "Look, can we agree that anything I tell you now will not become public knowledge?"

"I can't guarantee that if what you tell me proves important to our investigation. But if it doesn't then it will go no further."

Still Jackie hesitated. Kate had not allowed her and Beth Sandford to agree a way forward and so she had to make a decision on her own for both of them. Finally, she pursed her lips and blew them out. "I spent the evening with Beth Sandford in her rooms in the staff accommodation on site."

"Is this usual?"

"We have been in a relationship for a few months. We try and get together as often as we can. It's not easy for Beth to get away in an evening so I normally come back."

"What time did you arrive in her rooms?"

"About eightish. I have a key to Beth's rooms so I can creep in when it's quiet. I left again by midnight."

"I'm assuming no-one knows?"

"God, I hope not. Beth would have a fit. She is so worried about what other people will say. I've tried to tell her that people don't care these days but she is convinced she would lose everything."

"Thank you for your honesty. I know that can't have been easy."

"I don't mind but Beth does. I wish I could convince her but..." she shrugged before continuing, "I don't think she realises quite how

I feel. I think she thinks it is just an infatuation, but it isn't." This was said with determination. "I have had infatuations, and this… well, it's not that."

Kate smiled. "I won't take up any more of your time. I know free lessons must be very precious."

"Thank you." Jackie lifted up her bag and made to leave before turning back and saying, "Will you bear in mind what I've said about Beth, just in case…" again she tailed off.

"Just in case she's not as open as you have been?"

Jackie nodded.

"I will take everything into consideration."

Jackie smiled again and then sashayed out of the room. Kate smiled to herself. That was a very confident young woman.

CHAPTER 33

Following Jackie out into the foyer Kate watched her turn into the corridor before she walked across to the Head's office. She knocked firmly on the door and was immediately asked to enter. Beth Sandford was sat at the desk and was moving pieces of paper around in front of her. When she saw it was Kate she asked, "Do you know when they will release Elise's body? The trust is assuming that I will be arranging her funeral. Unless you know of family?"

Kate sat in the chair opposite Beth. She thought about Jack Newton. Would he want to have a say in his lover's funeral or would that be too public?

"I will check with the coroner about the release of the body. At this stage I don't know of any family but you might like to talk with Miss Hazel. She appears to have been a close friend."

Beth's hand went to her forehead. "Of course, Miss Hazel. I assume she now knows about Elise's death? I'd forgotten all about her. I should have gone and told her." She sounded genuinely upset that there had been this lapse on her part.

"I'm sure she would appreciate a visit, even now."

"Yes of course. And I will ask her for her ideas about the funeral. I think the trustees are thinking of something in Silstone's church rather than the chapel here."

She looked again at the papers in front of her and then back to Kate. "But that's not of interest to you, is it?"

Kate shrugged politely. "I assume it will be a large affair?"

"Oh yes. Past girls, some quite illustrious, parents and past parents and then of course staff and past staff and the trustees," with each group she referred to a separate piece of paper.

"Was Miss Betteridge particularly religious?"

"Although she attended the chapel service each month, which is C of E, I wouldn't say she had a strong religious faith." There was emphasis on the word 'religious', "but she did have a strong moral compass."

"Had you noticed any particular change in her over the last few months?" Kate was wondering how an affair with a married man could be squared with a 'strong moral compass'.

Beth Sandford closed her eyes before saying, "There was a spell before Christmas when she seemed to have something on her mind. I did actually ask her one evening. She'd invited me to her study for a drink. She did that from time to time, with some of the more senior staff."

"And what did she say?"

"She said she was just concerned that we might not reach our target for the fundraising. To be honest I wasn't totally convinced she was telling the truth, she knew we had some more promises to come in and we weren't far off the total. I wasn't convinced that was the true reason but to dig further would have been out of the question."

Kate thought Beth Sandford did look genuinely perplexed.

"Anyway, by the beginning of this term we had met the target and Elise seemed much happier in herself. So perhaps she told the truth after all."

Kate nodded and went to rise but then turned back, "By the way I meant to ask, where were you on the evening of Miss Betteridge's death?"

Beth Sandford gave a nervous laugh, "Once I finished the common room duty at eight thirty I went back to my rooms. I have a similar suite of rooms to Miss Betteridge's but in the staff block on the side of the quad."

"Were you there all evening?"

"Yes."

"Alone?"

Kate could see the calculations behind Beth Sandford's eyes. Finally, Kate saw that a decision had been made. "No. Having spoken with Jackie you will know that she was with me all evening. She left about midnight."

"Thank you for your honesty."

"Jackie says we should be more open about our relationship but I'm a very private person and, I suppose, I'm not sure how long Jackie will stay around. I know she's so much younger than me."

Kate was reluctant to play matchmaker but would it hurt to point Beth Sandford in the right direction? "I get the impression that Ms Fleet is a very determined and strong woman. I don't think she would settle for anything but what she wants."

CHAPTER 34

There being no sign of Colm as she exited Beth Sandford's office, she was just about to head for the exit when she had a thought. Gently knocking on Mrs Jessop's door she popped her head round. "I'm sorry to disturb you yet again but I have a question."

Mrs Jessop looked wary, "Yes?"

"Could you tell me where Kitty Hardcastle would be at this moment, please?"

This time Mrs Jessop called up something on her screen. Muttering to herself, "Kitty... Hardcastle. There! She looked up. She has a private study session so I would imagine she is in the library."

"The library."

Mrs Jessop patiently gave directions, "Right corridor, as far as you can go. That's the library."

As Kate was about to depart, Mrs Jessop added, "If she's not there she will be in the lower sixth common room. Come back on yourself to the stairs. Up to the second floor, turn left."

"Thank you, Mrs Jessop. You surely are the font of all knowledge."

Mrs Jessop smiled primly. Kate was sure Colm would have had a beam of a smile. Again the school was quiet as Kate made her way along the corridor but the silence in the library had layers. Kate looked along a row of study carrels. No sign of Kitty and then she saw her slouched in a soft chair over by one of the windows.

Kate made her way over and stood above Kitty and whispered, "Hi, Kitty, can I have a word?"

Kitty was startled and looked up, anxiety imprinted in every line. Kate hastened to reassure her, "You're not in trouble. I just need to clarify a point."

Warily, Kitty put down the book she had clasped to her breasts. "If we whisper we should be fine here."

"Okay," Kate agreed, keeping her voice soft. "On the night you were on the rota for Miss Betteridge's supper tray, did you prepare it for Izzy?"

Kitty looked surprised, "Prepare it? What do you mean?"

"Izzy said that when she went to the kitchen on the landing the tray was already laid with the cake cut and the chocolate ready. Even the milk was waiting in the jug. Did you do that?"

Kitty shook her head. "I suppose I should have thought about doing that… but no, I didn't."

"What about collecting it from Miss Betteridge later?"

Another shake of her head. "I was still at the task Ms Fleet had set us. I had to finish it back in my dorm."

"Do you know who did collect it? Izzy said

one of the girls offered so she didn't."

A frown appeared on Kitty's face, "Yes, I remember several girls said they would do it, but I don't know who did."

"Can you give me names?"

"To be honest I'm not sure I can. It would be one of the girls who was in the common room that evening. I could ask around and try and find out who was there?"

"That's fine. I just needed to check. I'll let you get back to studying. What are you reading?"

Kitty held up the book. It was one of the Asterix series. Kate smiled. "I remember reading them in French."

Kitty smiled nervously in reply, "Mine is in Latin. It's very easy but I just needed to have some down time without feeling like I was wasting time." She seemed to be asking for understanding.

"Sounds like a bright idea. Living in as well as being schooled here must make it quite intense at times."

Kitty smiled more fully and nodded her head. "Yes it's not always comfortable."

"Right I'll leave you to your studies," Kate winked as she left.

Out in the corridor two thoughts were uppermost in Kate's mind: judging by Kitty's surprise at her question, Izzy had not asked her about the supper tray and secondly Kate had also noticed that Kitty's left wrist was tightly bound and she was favouring it as she lifted the book to show Kate the title. Another accident?

Transcript Audio Log 2 mins 33 secs

They were back in again today. I don't know why but I wondered if it had anything to do with Kitty's accident last night, as the woman made a point of going to talk to her. I saw them in the library. I thought I'd planned it so well. No, I had planned it well it's just that Kitty must have nine lives, like her namesake's!

I made the excuse to Mum that I needed to go in and use the school library. I know she thinks I am a dedicated pupil so this caused no surprise. While almost everyone was in their common rooms or their house television rooms I slipped into Kitty's house and up to the landing where her room is. It's a good job she's in one of the older buildings because the ceilings in the top rooms are lower and there are single lightbulbs rather than strip lighting.

Using a chair from the stock room I unscrewed the bulb outside Kitty's room. In the stock room I also found an old rug. This was a much better idea. I had planned to push Kitty but they might have been able to detect that. This way she will just have tripped and fallen.

Later on, back at home, I told Mum I was going to spend the night with a friend. She doesn't like it but she thinks I work so hard I need a break. I slipped back into school and hid in the stock room in Kitty's House. I'd stayed there the night of Betty's death. There are so many small rooms in the older buildings that they don't know what to do with.

I curled up to sleep having set my mobile alarm. They say you are more disorientated if woken from a deep sleep and most people have their deepest sleeps between two and four. Using the torch on my phone I laid the rug at the top of the stairs and then I switched on the recording I'd made of a crying child. I waited on the landing until I saw the light under Kitty's door then I went down to the second landing and played the audio again. I heard Kitty's door open and the useless click of the light switch. I heard her trip and then a gasp of pain.

The audio had stopped and I could hear Kitty's heavy breathing punctuated with sobs. Somehow she has evaded me again. Frustrated I waited for her to go back to bed. I heard her tentatively take a few steps on the stairs and then stopped and returned. Her door shut and my plan had failed.

CHAPTER 35

Kate went and sat in the car and pulled out the other interviews the uniforms had conducted over the weekend. Briefly looking through she could see both Jackie's point about the ages of most of the staff but also evidence of Miss Betteridge's determination to appoint younger staff in the last seven years. No-one appeared to have a bad word to say about the victim but neither was there profuse plaudits.

Kate looked up as Colm skipped down the short flight of steps and trotted over to the car. "Sorry, boss. Have you been waiting long?"

"No, just casting an eye." She held up the sheaf of papers.

Colm nodded and settled himself into the car. Kate waited and when nothing was forthcoming asked, "So, what have you got?"

Colm reached into his inside pocket and pulled out his notebook. After a few seconds of flicking through the pages he gave a small cough. "Izzy Grey. According to Mrs Jessop every few weeks she comes to clean her computer. Apparently she plugs in a device," Colm turned to look directly at Kate, "From her description I would say it was a memory stick. According to Mrs Jessop, Izzy then spends about ten minutes reorganising documents and files." Colm leaned back, "But she wouldn't know whether Izzy was uploading a programme or downloading the contents of her computer."

There was a silence as each contemplated what it was Izzy Grey did with Mrs Jessop's computer. "If she has regular access to Mrs Jessop's computer then she has access to the entire school system," Kate surmised.

"And according to everyone I've spoken to Izzy is a genius with computers. Writes all her own programmes. What's to stop her from having uploaded some sort of spyware into the system?" Colm added.

"But why? Why would she want to have access to the school's system?"

"Could it be 'just because she can'?" Colm asked. "You know sometimes people who are good at something try out all sorts of weird things just to see if they can."

Kate looked out of the window. The rain had started again. Her instinct was that there was something here. Answering Colm's idea she said, "Izzy at twelve or so, may be. But she's seventeen now but she's still accessing whatever it is she's looking at."

Kate let her mind wander and then said, "We need one of the tech wizards in there. I'll square it with Beth Sandford but Mrs J mustn't know. I'll talk with Bart today and see what he can come up with."

Colm nodded and then flicked over a few

more pages. "Kitty (Katherine) Hardcastle. I managed to sweet talk the matron and got quite a bit of unofficial information. Kitty has always been prone to accidents; bruising her knees, spraining her ankle. You know the sort of thing?"

"But more than the other girls?"

"Yes. However, what is more interesting is the number of medical issues Kitty has had since last summer." Colm flicked again, "June of last year she had what they thought was food poisoning, just as she was due to take her early A-level exams."

"Anyone else have it?"

"No. Matron even let slip that she had wondered whether Kitty was just playing up, exam nerves, sort of thing, but she had to clean Kitty up and matron said there was no way she could have pretended that!"

Kate didn't let her mind dwell on that statement. "Did it impact on her exams?"

"Apparently not. As well as having access to the toilet, accompanied, when she wished, the school also sent in a medical note indicating her illness. Apparently she came out with A* in both languages."

"What else?"

"In the summer Kitty nearly drowned. Matron heard it from some of the girls who were there. Kitty had a beach party for her birthday at the beginning of September, just before term started. Apparently she's not a good swimmer so she was using an inflatable ring. Somehow an enormous hole appeared in it; it deflated at a point where Kitty was out of her depth. Not dramatically so but enough to make a non-swimmer panic. Fortunately, the lifeguard saw it all and had her back on dry land within minutes."

"Not really the sort of thing you can plan for is it?"

"Are you thinking that these are not accidents?"

"I really don't know. What else has poor Kitty been through?"

"In October there was the horse riding incident and just before Christmas the fall down the stairs."

"So in less than six months she has had four major health issues? Don't you think that's a lot?"

It was Colm's turn to look out of the window. "Taken individually you'd just think, bad luck, but when you put it like that it does seem a lot."

"And I noticed this morning that she's done something to her wrist."

Colm did another flick, "Yes, apparently the light on her dorm landing was out overnight and she tripped over the carpet. When she fell she tried to save herself and wrenched her wrist."

"Again. It sounds trivial but that's another incident."

Colm nodded and settled himself even more heavily into his seat in a self-satisfied way.

"Which is why I thought I'd take a look at the crime scene."

Kate turned and looked at him, "And?"

"There's no carpet there now. But, if the scuff marks are anything to go by, if Kitty had not saved herself she may well have tumbled down a steep set of stairs. Who knows what the outcome of that would have been?"

"Did you find out why she was up in the night?"

"No. I didn't think to ask. I assumed she needed the bathroom."

"I'm pretty sure that all the dorms are ensuite. I think I remember seeing it in the brochure last week, when we were on our way here."

"Do you think Kitty is in danger?"

Kate ran her fingers through her hair. A sure sign of frustration. "I really don't know but something is telling me that our murder, Kitty's accidents and Izzy's computer skills are all connected into something we don't yet know or understand."

CHAPTER 36

Colm was still looking through his notes. "I also happened to catch Mr Chapman on his way for a coffee in the staffroom and grabbed him. Hope that's okay?"

"Absolutely. What did he have to say?"

"Pretty much as Mrs Jessop reported. The girl concerned had tried cosying up to him and he had rejected her."

"Really? Nubile young woman offering herself?"

"No, honestly. He seemed genuinely embarrassed by it. I don't think he realises how desirable he is to the opposite sex."

"So what happened next?"

"Then she turned the tables and threatened to report him for improper behaviour. He called her bluff but made a point of reporting it to his Head of Department who in turn let the Head know."

"Could he have got his version in first to blunt her actions?"

"What a sort of double bluff. 'If I tell them about it they won't believe the girl'?" Colm stared out of the window and seemed lost in thought. Finally he spoke, "No, I don't think so."

"What about his wife's actions?"

Colm smiled, "Reading between the lines I

would say she is a bit of a loose cannon. Is always out to protect him so that he can get on with his art. She thinks he is the next Francis Bacon. He thinks he just needs a chance."

"What about the night of the murder?"

"Left school about five. He had an after school art group, still with a chaperone. He and his wife live on the far side of the town so it's normally about a twenty minute journey but he says the lights were out on King Street and traffic was bad, so it was closer to six before he got in."

"Well we can check that, can't we? The lights?"

Colm nodded and continued. "He says he went to get changed into his painting gear and was fiddling with a piece until his wife got in at about seven. The pair of them then cooked, ate and she settled down to watch telly and he went back to his work."

"So not likely that he was in the kitchenette preparing the tray, unless it was done much earlier but surely someone else would have seen it. Dr Heath said it was not set up when she went in about five fifteen."

"He says he worked until just before eleven when his wife came up and reminded him what the time was."

"So they alibi each other. We'll need to talk to the wife but it doesn't feel right, does it?"

Colm shook his head as he closed his notebook. "Trouble is no-one feels right."

Kate sighed. She agreed. Nothing was shaking loose. Now into this she had Kitty and Izzy. How did they fit into this? Did they fit in? Was she obsessing on something peripheral happening in the school? Why did Kitty's 'accidents' worry her?

"Shall we track down Judith Chapman or straight back to the station?" Colm broke into her thoughts.

"Yes, let's talk to Mrs Chapman. Do you know where we'll find her now?"

Colm checked his notes again. "She's on a half day today so she should be home."

"Okay, let's go."

CHAPTER 37

Kate's thoughts flew around her head as Colm steadily drove them back into town. Was Kitty in danger? Danger as in another murder? It was all so nebulous and yet she was sure it was all connected. Would Kitty survive another night? The 'accidents' seemed to be happening more frequently.

"Sorry. Colm, pull over when you can."

Unquestioningly, Colm waited and then pulled into the entrance to a farmer's field.

"I may have this all wrong but if something were to happen to Kitty overnight I would be guilty of gross negligence. I'm going to see if Bart is available. I want one of our techs in and Kitty out of there today, if possible."

Colm waited patiently while Kate dialled and waited to be connected. "Hello, Sian? It's Kate Medlar. Is Bart available at all in the next hour?" There was a pause and then, "Great I'll be with you in half-an-hour. Thanks Sian."

"You do know," said Colm conversationally, "That if anyone else refers to him as Bart they get a verbal rap on the knuckles from Sian?"

Kate smiled. She and Sian had hit it off from their first meeting. She thought Sian felt there was too much testosterone around the station at times and so took every opportunity to challenge it.

Getting no reply, Colm continued, "So we're back to the station?"

"Yes please, Colm."

After a few minutes, while Colm got them onto the right road, Kate said, "While I'm talking to Bart will you contact Terry and find out where they are with their Phipps case?"

Colm hesitated, "Terry said he'd be in touch when he had news." He glanced over, "We wouldn't like it if someone was chasing us up would we?"

Kate grimaced. Colm was right. She'd be livid if someone she was doing a favour for began to snap at her heels. She sighed. "Yes, you're right."

As they drove into the station car park Kate said, "Before I go in to see Bart do you think I'm over reacting to this Kitty thing, honestly?"

Colm parked, turned the engine off and sat. Finally he said, "At first I thought Kitty was just clumsy and/or unlucky but when you see it laid out it does seem to be far more than accidental. I can't see what the connection is but I'm also worried about her."

***

Kate wished she had Colm's support as she saw the sceptical look on Bart's face as she unveiled what he obviously thought was her half-baked idea. He had been signing papers as she spoke but now he put his pen down and looked over his glasses at her. "You think this girl's accidents are something more sinister? So what is the killer's motive?"

Kate held her nerve, "Yes, sir. I don't know what the motive is, yet, but we can't find a motive for Elise's Betteridge's death either but it happened."

"So what are you proposing to do?"

"I want to suggest to the acting Head that Kitty needs to go home for a week or so. Between us we'll come up with a reason so as not to worry her parents.

"And the Head will go along with this?"

"Yes, I think so." Kate crossed her fingers.

"And then we have the maverick computer genius? You want one of our tech guys to go in, under cover, to look at the school's systems? What are you hoping to find?"

Kate reiterated her idea, "I believe the girl has been monitoring the school systems. I'm hoping one of our techies will be able to trace where she's been and what she's been doing."

"And this is based on the secretary's statement that the girl regularly cleans up her machine?"

"Yes, sir."

The scepticism had not left his face. "All of this is based on your instincts? You have no evidence?"

Kate was waiting for the guillotine to drop.

Well, if Bart wouldn't support her she would at least warn Beth Sandford about her worries over Kitty.

Bart ran his hands over his balding head, just settling a few stray wisps. "I'll meet you half way, Kate. You can have Constable Zara Bakir from the tech unit. She's comparatively new so no-one should clock her as police. You'll have to come up with a reason why she's there if you're not going to tip your genius off. But the other girl, I think you need to talk to the Head and see what her response is. I'm not giving official sanction to her need to go home."

A little flutter of joy made its presence felt under her breast bone. She would be able to convince Beth Sandford that they needed to do something and a woman from tech would be perfect. "Thank you sir."

"I hope that Bakir is able to find something, otherwise it is going to be hard to justify the use of her time."

"Yes, sir. May I go and see if I can catch her now?"

Bart waved his hand in dismissal. As Kate was about to close the door he called after her, "We do need a result on this Kate, and soon."

Kate nodded.

CHAPTER 38

Constable Zara Bakir had been delighted to have a change of scene and also came up with a plausible reason for her being there: in case the American merger still went ahead she was there to check on the school's existing IT system. She would get a colleague, who could do a good American accent, to ring and ask for Beth Sandford once Kate was there. Mrs Jessop would not be told the truth but the subterfuge gave veracity to Zara's cover story.

"The main thing is you need to be really careful as we don't know what kind of device, if any, this girl has loaded onto the system. For all we know she may have an early warning system."

Zara smiled, "Don't worry, ma'am. I will tread as lightly as a tiptoeing butterfly!"

Kate had to laugh at the simile. "That and more. Don't underestimate this girl. She may be still at school but I'm told she's a genius."

Zara nodded solemnly, "In this field the younger you are the better you are. Will I need some form of ID do you think?"

"That might be an idea." Kate jotted down the name of the American college involved with Blaiseforth. "They must have a website, see what you can come up with."

They left Zara happily, designing her business card.

***

Heading back to the school Kate felt a need to get Kitty into a safe place and so rang ahead and asked Mrs Jessop to have Kitty in the Head's office for when she arrived.

"You really think she is in imminent danger?" Colm enquired.

"I just think whoever is doing this is ramping things up and I don't want to risk her life by being too cautious."

Colm shrugged. "How did Bart take it?"

Kate smiled thinly, "A bit like you. Wants to believe that I haven't lost my mind, despite the rubbish that's coming out of my mouth!"

Colm laughed, "I believe in you, boss. I just can't see the motive."

"Me neither!"

As they drove up the school drive the Manor looked inviting with windows ablaze and shadows of people walking behind large windows. Kate checked her watch, barely four but the winter days were short and on wet ones like today dusk was teatime.

Mrs Jessop must have been looking out for them because she appeared from her office as Kate and Colm entered the foyer.

"Detective Inspector, I have placed Kitty in the Head's office. Poor girl, she's scared to death that she's in serious trouble and I couldn't give her any comfort because I didn't know why you wanted to see her."

"Kate ignored the inferred complaint and question, "Thank you Mrs Jessop. Is Miss Sandford in her office?"

"No. She said she would return for four thirty. She's taking one of the after school classes."

"That's no problem." Colm stepped in, "Could we trouble you for tea for all four of us at four thirty, Mrs Jessop?" He gave her a smile as he followed Kate across the floor.

Kate opened the door into the office. Kitty was curled into one of the soft chairs to one side of the room. She looked up and Kate saw her naked fear. Now was she afraid of why she was there or because she was also wondering about her 'accidents'?

"Hi, Kitty. Don't look so worried, you're not in trouble." Kate tried to sound calm.

Kitty's shoulders relaxed a little but there was still a great deal of tension being held in check, Kate decided.

She sat in a chair opposite Kitty and Colm sat, out of Kitty's eye line, on one of the chairs around the meeting table. As an opener Kate asked, "How's your wrist? I noticed earlier it was bound up."

Kitty looked at her wrist and back to Kate, "I slipped."

"I think it was something a bit more than a slip, wasn't it?"

Kitty looked at her sharply. "My usual clumsy self. Tripped over a rug and fell. I grabbed the banister as I fell and wrenched my wrist."

"You poor thing. When was this?" Kate kept her tone light, conversational.

"Yesterday. Well more accurately during the night."

"I can't see you as a picnic at midnight in the dorm, kind of girl!"

"No." She sighed deeply. "I haven't told anyone because they didn't believe me before when I said I tripped over something. I thought I heard someone crying on the landing outside my dorm last night."

Kate gave her a nod of encouragement.

"When I looked out I couldn't see anyone and when I tried to switch the light on, the bulb must have blown. I could still hear the crying so I headed across the landing. That's when I tripped over a rug." She paused and then said defiantly, "It felt like a rug but there shouldn't have been one there. And then there wasn't one there this morning."

"So what do you think happened?" Kate asked calmly.

Kitty sighed, "I really don't know. I'm sure there was a rug," but her tone gave away her self-doubt.

"What would you say if I said I believe you?" Kate asked.

Kitty looked directly at Kate and went very still. Kate was sure a lot of calculations were going on behind the marble features. Then silent tears oozed out of Kitty's eyes. She did nothing to wipe them away and they began to drip onto her sweatshirt, leaving a damp trail. Finally, Kitty sat up straighter, "You believe me? You know that someone is trying to hurt me?"

Now it was Kate's turn to calculate, "I believe that you have had more than your fair share of accidents in the last few months."

Kitty's silent tears turned to gasping sobs. Kate leant across and held the hand of the unharmed wrist and pulled a box of tissues off the coffee table to one side. Kitty groped and grabbed a handful and clumsily tried to stem the flow of tears. Slowly her breathing evened out and she removed her hand from Kate's.

"I think you need to go home for a few days."

"Please don't tell them. They've sacrificed so much to get me here."

Stalling the look of horror on Kitty's face, Kate continued, "We'll get Miss Sandford to ring them and explain that with the death of Miss Betteridge and these accidents she thinks you need a break."

Kitty nodded slowly. "It's half term next week as well."

"Even better. Do your parents live far from here?"

Kitty gave a watery smile, "No, just the other side of Eashire." Seeing the query in Kate's gaze she continued, "Mum and Dad wanted me to have the full Blaiseforth experience so they made me a boarder."

Further conversation was prevented by the arrival of Miss Sandford.

CHAPTER 39

"Detective Inspector, I understand you wanted to see me about an urgent matter." Her eyes went to Kitty and her right eyebrow went up. "Kitty, are you all right?"

Kate answered, "We've been discussing the number of accidents that Kitty has experienced just lately and we think she needs to go home for a few days and then into half term."

Miss Sandford began to form a response but whether it was the tone of Kate's voice or the look on Kitty's face she remained silent and then addressed Kitty, "Is that what you want, Kitty?"

Barely above a whisper, Kitty answered, "Yes, please."

Miss Sandford made a decision and went and sat behind the desk. She jolted the screen into life and clicked through several settings before reaching for the telephone on her desk.

"Mrs Hardcastle? Beth Sandford here."

A pause.

"No I am fine but I am a little worried about Kitty. She's in good health but I think the whole situation with Miss Betteridge's death and the police enquiry has unsettled her."

Another pause.

"Yes. I agree. Last night she had a fall and I think it was as a result of sleep walking, a sure sign of emotional distress."

A longer pause.

"Oh did she? Well that confirms my thoughts. I think she needs to leave for the February half term early. Are you able to collect her this evening?"

The room could hear the voice of Mrs Hardcastle calling her husband and then, "Half-an-hour. Perfect. I'll see you then."

Without looking at anyone in the room Miss Sandford pressed the receiver rest and redialled. "Fay? Would you come to my office and collect Kitty Hardcastle, please? She's going to go home tonight and will need to pack a bag and collect work. With her damaged wrist she's going to need a hand."

"Yes, thank you."

"Right, Kitty. "Don't take too much work home. I do genuinely think you need a rest."

"What about the Blaiseforth prize?" Kitty's face was suddenly deeply etched with worry.

"This will have no bearing. That's the last thing you need to worry about."

A knock at the door heralded the arrival of Fay. A small wiry woman popped her head round the door. Colm smiled, "Matron, how lovely to see you again."

Fay moved into the room and smiled back, "And you DC Hunter." Then she turned to Kitty. "Come on then, Kitty. Let's get you sorted. I think this is an excellent idea."

Kitty grabbed the school bag at her feet and made her way out of the room. Matron placed a motherly arm across her shoulders as they left.

As the door closed Beth Sandford turned blazing eyes on Kate. "Would you mind telling me what is going on? You come into my school and I know you have tried to keep a low profile but your very presence has set the school a buzz and now this." Indicating the departed figure.

Kate came and sat in front of the desk and hunched forward with her arms on the desk. "Miss Sandford, Beth, I sincerely apologise for having to take such high handed actions."

Some of the tension left Beth Sandford's body and Kate continued, "I may be over reacting but I think that Kitty is being targeted. I don't know who by and I don't know why. I don't even know if it is connected with Miss Betteridge's death but I felt Kitty was in danger."

Beth Sandford sat back in her chair, "Coincidentally Fay and I had a discussion earlier today on the number of accidents Kitty has had recently and that most of them could have been very serious, if not tragic. That is the reason why I went along with this charade."

"I'm afraid more charades are about to be enacted," Kate said.

Beth Sandford sighed, "Tell me the worst."

"In a while a colleague of ours will ring the school claiming to be an American connected to the college Miss Betteridge was in negotiations with."

"And the purpose of such a claim."

"I would like to bring in one of my colleagues to survey your IT system."

Miss Sandford actually spluttered, "You want to do what?"

"I believe you may have some spyware in your system and I want to know what it does."

"Why on earth... Is this connected to Elise's death?"

"Again, I'm not sure."

"Tell me DI Medlar, why should I put up with any more interference from you?"

Kate leant back in her chair and raised her hands palms up and flat. "I believe all these elements are connected. I have no evidence and to be perfectly honest with you if you contacted my superior, DCI Bartholomew, and objected I think he would support you."

Kate's honesty took Miss Sandford's breath away. Her fingers tapped restlessly on the arm of her chair. She looked like she was about to respond when the telephone rung.

Kate held her breath. Now they would know if Beth Sandford was on board.

"Yes, ...oh indeed." Beth looked towards Kate. "Yes, put him through."

Kate heard the click as the caller was put through. Colm was already out of the door and Kate heard Mrs Jessop's office door open and close.

Beth listened for a few seconds and then passed the receiver to Kate, "I think he does a terrible accent."

"DI Medlar here."

A deep voice replied. "Okay boss. Anything else you need?"

"No, thanks Max."

Colm slipped back into the room and returned to his seat. He gave Kate the thumbs up. Beth noticed. "I'm assuming Mrs Jessop is not to know?"

Kate nodded.

"You surely can't suspect her? She barely knows the part of the system she uses."

"No. I am quite sure Mrs Jessop is not involved but she may, unwittingly, give away what we are doing. So better for her not to know. How would you convey the information that someone is going to be working in her office? Call her in? Go into her?"

Beth Sandford rose. "I think I need to tell her in person. Excuse me." She strode across the room and let herself quietly out.

"Phew! I thought we were shipwrecked before we'd set sail, then," Colm said.

"Umm. It's why I was totally honest with her. How did you distract Mrs J?"

"I asked for more biscuits. I pulled the, haven't stopped for lunch routine. As I walked in, her finger was hovering over the switch on the phone. I think she was tempted to eavesdrop."

"Good thinking. And sorry about lunch. I'll treat you to fish and chips on the way back."

"Thanks, boss."

CHAPTER 40

Miss Sandford walked back in. "The Hardcastles have just driven up. Would you wait in the meeting room whilst I see them? I don't want your presence muddying the water."

"Not a problem." Kate and Colm rose and stepped across the foyer to the meeting room. "Leave the light off, Colm. I want to be a curtain twitcher."

They both stepped over to within a few feet of the window and watched as a middle aged couple walked across the drive. They both looked like college lecturers: tidily dressed but not particularly fashionable. Comfortable in their own skins, was Kate's verdict.

Once they'd disappeared into the building they sat still in the dark. Kate yawned and rubbed her eyes tiredly. "God. I hope I've got this right."

"What? Kitty?"

"Yes," a pause, "No. The more I think about it the more I'm sure she's in danger if she stays. I'm worried about the IT bit. The bit that Bart could have my guts for. That's the long shot. Am I over thinking it? Has it got anything to do with our victim's death? That seems to have faded into the background. Just one break through. Just one tiny bit of evidence."

Colm remained silent and then commented, "They're leaving." Again they both stood and watched. Kitty was tucked under the arm of her Dad and held close whilst her Mum held her hand. For a moment, just before she ducked into the back of the car Kitty looked across its roof and seemed to Kate to look directly at her. Kate felt something relax within her chest. "Well at least this bit is sorted."

They watched until the Hardcastles drove away.

"Right, let's go and check that Beth Sandford is really on board." As she made her way out of the room Kate stopped and turned back to Colm following closely behind. "Tell you what. Have another natter with Mrs J and find out what Izzy gets up to in the holidays."

Colm nodded and veered off to reception and Kate crossed to the Head's office. She knocked on the door and thought it politic to wait until given permission to enter. The command came.

Beth Sandford was watching the Hardcastles drive away from the Manor. As the glare of their red tail lights disappeared she turned away from the window and sat in one of the comfy chairs. She indicated for Kate to sit where Kitty had sat.

"This is all very perplexing," she waved a hand generally in the air.

"I agreed with Kitty going home because for some reason she is having a lot of accidents and when I spoke to her mother she said Kitty is more accident prone when anxious and when younger would sleep walk. All these factors supported Kitty's need for some time away from the school."

All of this was said matter-of-factly but then her voice took on more energy, "I cannot believe that someone, in this school," said with emphasis, "is deliberately targeting Kitty to do her harm." She looked pointedly at Kate.

Kate eased back into her seat. "I can only repeat what I said earlier: that I was concerned about Kitty's safety here in school. The reasons you have just given may well account for all the incidents. Either way I am pleased she has gone home to her family.

"What I am less comfortable or convinced of is the idea that Izzy Grey..." Kate went to interrupt but Beth Sandford spoke over her protestations, "Please, Inspector, give me some credit for intelligence. The only one who has access to the school system and could imbed some kind of spyware programme is Izzy Grey. I know she regularly helps Barbara with her computer."

Kate tactfully agreed with Beth Sandford's surmise. "Yes. I know it sounds bizarre but we are unable to find anything in Miss Betteridge's life that would account for her death. I am just trying to follow every possible lead."

"I really don't think Izzy Grey is your murderer. Surely the fact that she took the tray in would immediately cast suspicion on her?"

"It did. But it could be a double bluff."

Beth Sandford snorted in derision. "I have said to Barbara that your tech person will only be a couple of days. Will that be sufficient?"

Kate hadn't got a clue but said, "Hopefully, yes."

"In that case before I go to monitor the girls' supper I need to contact Ken Grant about the American college sending someone in. It would be a courtesy, at least, and given my acting status I think I should."

Kate agreed, "I'll get out of your hair now, then. Constable Bakir will be here at nine tomorrow. And if at all possible I will try not to be here!" Kate rose and headed towards the door.

Beth Sandford called after her, "I understand you are trying to do your job. I just feel you have got it wrong."

Kate nodded and closed the door behind her. She hoped to God she hadn't got it all wrong.

Transcript Audio Log 13secs

Rumour has it that Kitty has gone home. No-one is sure whether she asked or was sent or whether she is coming back. Could I really have got rid of her? Well now I need to move on to the other one. The police have already interviewed her and I'm sure she's under suspicion so let's make that more concrete.

CHAPTER 41

When Kate got in the following morning it was to a note from Mike Edwards asking her to pop into the forensic suite when she had a moment. Meeting Colm on the stairs she took him with her. The forensic suite – although a group of interconnecting rooms would be a more accurate term – was busy with a range of tasks. Kate spotted Mike at his desk and called hello as she made her way towards him.

"Ah, morning Kate, Colm. Just an update of your footage from the school." He wandered over to a large computer screen bounded by all sorts of digital and electrical gizmos. "To be honest, not a lot. But I thought this was interesting."

He had keyed the footage to the place he wanted to show. It was a view from the top of one of the gate posts to the drive. The time indicated eight zero nine on the Monday night of their victim's death. A car drove in. The scene then switched to the main car park at the front of the school. Time eight ten, eight eleven, Miles let the machine slip to eight fifteen. No car had appeared.

"Where did the car go?" Colm asked.

Mike shrugged. "Exactly. Where did the car go?"

Kate thought she knew the answer but asked,

"Is there a shot where we can see the number plate?"

Mike rewound to the first view. The lights at the gate gave some illumination to the rear number plate and they could clearly make out, J94 FLE. "It's a private plate," Miles observed.

"Yes. I think I know who that belongs to. Unfortunately, I am also pretty sure it has nothing to do with our case."

"Sorry, Kate. That's the only nugget I have so far. We're still going through the quad cameras."

"Thanks, Mike. By the way, how did the discussion with Bart go?"

Mike grinned broadly, he definitely looked like the cat who got the cream. "He said, yes. Apparently there is a police fund he can access for using new methods on existing crimes."

Kate returned his grin. "That's brilliant. So how long are we looking at for some results?"

Mike's grin dropped, "Unfortunately, we're looking at three to four weeks."

Kate stood up taller, "Well, hopefully we will have cracked it before then but it is good to know we may have some supporting evidence."

As they left the suite Colm asked, "So who does the car belong to, boss?"

"I think its Jackie Fleet. She obviously has a secret car parking place on the evenings she visits Beth Sandford."

"Oh, of course," Colm sighed. "Nothing is coming loose, is it boss?"

"No, and I don't think Bart will wait four weeks for his answer."

Back in their incident room Alice called out, "Morning ma'am. Constable Bakir has just rung in to say that she has already found something but that the butterfly has not been detected!" Her confusion at the message evident on her face.

Kate and Colm both laughed. Kate took pity on Alice's pensive look, "It just means her access to the computer system hasn't set off any warning bells."

"Oh, right."

Kate could hear the shrug of indifference in her tone as she searched her desk for the report on Jack Newton.

"Alice, do you know where Len has put his report on Jack Newton? I want a quick look before we interview him this morning."

Alice pulled a file off her own desk and passed it to Kate. It took Kate only a few minutes to realise that the orderly compilation of the report was on the same lines as the other work Alice had done.

"Alice, why didn't Len compile this report?" Alice looked up and Kate continued, "Please don't deny it. Your reports have their own style. This..." waving the manila file, "is not Len's work."

"I... Len said he was snowed under with the other work you'd set him, so I took it on."

"What other work? The only thing I set him was some research on the American college. And that was Saturday's work. I haven't seen that either." Kate could feel herself getting angry.

At that moment Sergeant Hughes stepped up to her desk, "Excuse me, ma'am."

Kate was about to snap a response but looked up and saw a concerned look on his face. He continued, "Just wanted to check something you've written here." He handed her a blank piece of paper.

Kate was astute enough to know that Hughes was sending a message; one she could clearly read. "Sorry, that's meant to be an 'e'."

"Thank you, ma'am."

"Alice," PC Giles turned around with some reluctance. "Thank you for the report. Would you ask Len to be here for a team briefing at lunchtime, please?"

"Yes, ma'am."

"Thank you."

CHAPTER 42

Colm and Kate had gone through the report on Jack Newton and discussed the points they wanted to clarify. Jack Newton was a retired civil engineer who had worked for a large corporation and had travelled far and wide on their ticket. He was an Eashire man, born and bred and had returned to his roots when he'd retired. He and his wife had lived in their house in St Catherine's Close a little under five years.

Pulling up outside his house Kate noted two things; one that Jodie Prince's curtain twitched as they drew up and that a five year old, pale blue Fiat 500 was now on the drive of number 32. Mr Newton had clearly been waiting for them as the door opened before Kate had lifted her hand to knock. She and Colm both displayed their warrant cards but Mr Newton barely glanced at them.

"Come in. Come in."

The hallway was warm and smelt pleasantly of furniture polish that reminded Kate of her mum. "Let me take your coats and then go on into the living room." Newton helped Kate with her jacket and took Colm's. As he hung them on the pegs behind the front door he said, "I've got the kettle on. Tea?"

"Thank you."

"Right go on in and get comfortable and I won't be a minute." With that Newton bustled down the hall to the kitchen at the end.

The living room was even more redolent of polish and Kate could see the tracks left by the vacuum cleaner in the carpet. The room was long and thin. The back part was set up as a dining room with a sideboard and display cabinet. There were French doors that opened onto a pristine patio area. The living room had the usual three piece suite, TV and bureau in the window. Pictures scattered every surface and trailed across the mantelpiece.

Jack Newton had changed very little according to his wedding photograph. Tall and broad shouldered but he had not let himself run to fat. The once dark hair was now grey and perhaps a little thinner but other than that, easily recognisable. The photographs chronicled the life he and his wife had led. Holidays and special occasions. But if time had been kind to Jack Newton not so to his wife. In her wedding photograph she was petite and vibrant but in, what Kate considered, the latest photograph, she was small, dumpy and the vitality had left her eyes.

Two generations of the Newton family were also on display. An only girl, the baby photo, followed by numerous school ones and then her wedding day. This in turn was followed by two baby photographs and then the progress of another young girl. It was this photograph Kate was looking at as Jack Newton came back in carrying a tea tray.

"That's my grand-daughter, Chloe. Mind you that's about five years out of date. She's going through that phase when she won't be photographed."

Placing the tray carefully onto the coffee table in front of the three seater sofa he said, "Help yourselves." He then took a mug from the tray, already poured.

Starting gently Kate asked, "How long have you lived here, Mr Newton?"

"Call me, Jack. My wife, Audrey and I moved in nearly five years ago. Just before Audrey got her diagnosis of Alzheimer's. She's at The Orchards now." His face had taken on a wistful look. "It's an unkind illness. They disappear before your eyes." He then shook himself and sat up straighter. "But its Elise you want to talk about isn't it? I know she's dead, if that's what you came to tell me. A heart attack."

Kate let the cause of death go unchallenged, "How long had you known Miss Betteridge?"

"We met on the second Sunday of June last year." There was a pause which Kate did not fill. Thinking he would want to continue. "I met her at The Orchard, where my wife is. His face grew sadder. "Audrey was having a…" he seemed to be groping for the best description and settled for, "a bad day. The care staff suggested I go and have a coffee and let Audrey settle."

He turned to them, "I don't know if you know but The Orchards has a little mall as part of the complex. There's a hairdressers, chiropodist and a little café." He reminisced and smiled. "I was so full of my own woes when I went in that I didn't see Elise and Miss Hazel. It was Miss Hazel who called me over and so I sat with them." He shook his head, almost in wonder, "I can't remember what we chatted about now but I had such a good time and somehow we made arrangements to meet again the following Sunday."

"So did you only meet on Sundays, sir and at The Orchards?" Colm asked.

Jack nodded his head. "Sunday was the best day for Elise to get away from the school but we soon began to play hooky." His eyes twinkled. "We had such a great deal in common. She was a wonderful woman," and his eyes pooled.

Kate coughed and uncharacteristically felt a little embarrassed to ask her next question. "Did your relationship develop further?"

Jack looked at her levelly. "Did we become lovers? No. I love my wife and would never do that to her. Elise and I came to a decision, just before Christmas, that we would enjoy our deep friendship but we would not, how do they say it today? Go to the next stage? I think that for Elise her moral compass was also very unsettled about where our friendship was going."

"Did anyone else know about your friendship

with Elise?" Kate asked.

"I told my daughter, Megan, at Christmas."

"How did she take it, sir?"

Jack gave a watery smile, "She was wonderful. She even went on to say that she would understand if I wanted to have an affair. But I told her I wouldn't do that to her mum."

"Was it Megan you went to see at the weekend?" Kate asked.

"Yes. I knew she'd understand how I was feeling."

"Could we have your daughter's contact details, sir?"

"Yes of course. She'll be home at the moment, why not give her a ring." He fumbled in his trouser pocket for his mobile and found and read out a mobile number. Colm keyed it into his own phone and then went outside.

"Now," Jack said flatly, "are you able to tell me why all these questions about Elise? I am assuming that there is something more than a heart attack behind your questions?"

Kate repeated her mantra, "The post-mortem showed up some inconsistences which we are trying to get answers to."

Jack's face went white. "I'm not a stupid man, Inspector, and I do watch a lot of crime drama," another weak smile, "but are you saying that Elise may have been murdered?"

"Honestly, sir. That is what we are trying to find out. I have to ask you, where were you on

Monday evening between six and ten, last week?"

"I got back from sitting with Audrey about six thirty, I think. Then I was here, and by ten I was worried about Elise." Kate cocked an eyebrow and Jack explained. "Elise and I had got into the habit of phoning at about nine-thirty each evening for a chat. Sometimes it would be mere minutes and other times we could be on the phone for half-an-hour or more."

Not letting on that she already knew the answer, Kate continued, "So what did you do when Elise didn't phone?"

"First I sent a text, thinking she'd got caught up with something and a bit later on I phoned but it rang out to the voicemail."

"Did you leave a message?"

"No. I wasn't sure I should. I'm sorry that makes it sound very furtive, doesn't it."

"So when did you find out that Elise had died?"

"I contacted the school, about ten o'clock, I was at my wit's end. I pretended to be a potential parent wanting to talk to the Head. A very nice lady told me what had happened." Tears this time made it over the ledge of his eyes and tracked down his cheeks.

"I'm sorry to ask this but can you think of anyone or any reason why someone would want to harm Elise?"

Most people instantly answer, 'No', but Jack Newton stopped and thought. Then shaking his head he said, "I really can't. She was the headmistress of a prestigious girls' school. That was her life. Why would anyone want to kill her?" The tears were now flowing freely.

Kate got up and motioned for Jack to stay sat. "I am genuinely sorry for your loss, Jack."

CHAPTER 43

Colm was just finishing up his call when Kate exited number 32 with his jacket over her arm. "All pan out?"

"Yep. She thought it was great that her dad had someone to go out and about with and he was distraught when he arrived on Wednesday. She said, 'It's like he's lost two women he's loved'."

"Umm. Miss Hazel said a similar thing. So what's your impression?"

"Nah. It's not him."

Kate had to agree. So it wasn't passion. Back to money. She wondered how Zara Bakir was getting on. "Okay. We could go and see Judith Chapman. Do you have contact details for her?"

A few moments later Colm was talking to Judith Chapman. "That would be fine. Thank you Mrs Chapman we will be with you in the next twenty minutes or so."

"Where are we meeting her?" Kate asked.

"At their home. She's taken the day off to start preparing her husband's paintings for an exhibition he's mounting in the Tourist Information Centre."

***

A little under twenty minutes later Colm parked outside a 1960s council house. The whole area had that slightly run down, missing the latest sparkle, kind of air. The Chapman's house looked no more neglected than the others but no attempt had been made at maintaining a garden.

After a smart rap Judith Chapman opened the flaking door. She was mid to late twenties with a slightly anxious look to her eyes. Kate and Colm held up their warrant cards. Without a word Mrs Chapman stepped back and allowed them to follow her into the house. The front door opened directly into the living room with a set of stairs to the right. The furniture was practical but would win no prizes in the fashion or beauty stakes.

Judith Chapman sat on a spongy looking sofa and pointed to the matching chairs. "I know you've spoken with Matt. He would never harm a fly. Even though that woman was investigating him." Her tone was aggressive and aggrieved.

"We understand that Miss Betteridge was quite happy that your husband had done nothing wrong but had to investigate the girl's claim. Especially with all the media coverage of institutions covering up sexual abuse. Didn't you see that?"

Judith Chapman gave a derisive sniff, "Her and the reputation of the school," she sneered. "What about Matt's reputation?"

"I wasn't aware that anyone outside of the parties concerned were aware of the problem. It certainly was not mentioned in any of the statements that were taken."

"That's as may be. What would happen if it did get out? Matt's only working there whilst he gets his name known in the right circles. Last thing he needs is for that kind of rumour to start circulating."

"Is that what you went to see Miss Betteridge about?"

Judith Chapman did have the good grace to blush. She looked down at her hands. "I admit I blew up when I should have thought more about it. I was just so angry on Matt's behalf. He is so mild mannered he would never say anything."

"What about the threat you made as you left?"

"What threat?" She seemed puzzled by this accusation.

Colm leafed through his notes. "You were heard to say something like, 'You'll pay for this'."

Judith Chapman shook her head, "I don't remember saying that. It was probably just something to say. You know? In the heat of the moment!" Now she did look worried. "Look I know there's something fishy about Miss Betteridge's death, but I didn't do anything to her. I was just letting off steam."

Kate believed her but continued with her questioning. "Would you take us through your movements last Monday evening, please?"

Judith Chapman took in a deep breath and began. "I left work a few minutes after six to catch the six ten bus from Bridge Street. I work at Tameworth's Dentistry. The bus was a few minutes late and it's normally about a fifteen minute journey but there were problems with the traffic lights at King Street and we were stuck there for quite some time. I got off at the corner of this road and walked home. I think it was just after seven when I got in."

"Did you contact your husband to tell him you would be late?" Kate asked.

"No. My finishing times are a bit of a moveable feast. It depends how late Mr Tameworth runs over. Technically his last appointment is five thirty but he always over runs. Anyway, Matt would be in his studio and time becomes unimportant when he is there."

"So what did you do for the evening? It must be hard having to cook once you're home if you're that late?" Colm suggested.

Judith Chapman shrugged, "We normally cook together and it's never very exciting. By eight we had eaten and washed up. Matthew went back to his studio and I watched the telly."

"Anything in particular?"

"What? On the telly?"

Kate nodded.

"Um. I watched Bake Off. I can't cook but I love watching ordinary people doing their best. Then I think it was a documentary about Egypt. I've always wanted to go there. I watched the news and then a comedy thing before heading for bed about eleven."

"And did either of you go out at all during the evening?"

"Nope!"

Kate flipped her own notebook shut and stood. Colm followed suit. "Thank you Mrs Chapman."

As they walked back to the car Kate sent Colm an inquisitive look. He shook his head. "Nah!"

CHAPTER 44

Back at the station they each began their allotted tasks. Words blurred before Kate's eyes. She could hear Colm huffing his way through the report on their victim. At midday they had a short briefing where she gave an update on their interview with Jack Newton. Alice had completed the financial search on the Hardcastles.

"He is a lecturer at the technical college and she is the heritage manager for Eashire. She's based at the museum in town but also has responsibility for the ruins of the castle. Nearly six years ago they sold a very nice Victorian villa out towards Westergate and bought a modern semi, three bedroom on that newish estate on the Calford Road. As far as I can see the capital they received has gone into an account that pays for putting Kitty through Blaiseforth Manor. According to their bank there is talk about re-mortgaging their present house, I suppose to get Kitty through university."

Kate puffed out her cheeks. "I understand what Kitty meant when she said they'd sacrificed so much. Where was Kitty before Blaiseforth?"

Alice checked her notes. "She attended Camworth Primary School."

Kate raised an eyebrow, "I thought they lived

out towards Westergate?"

"They did but Camworth Primary takes from quite a large catchment that includes Westergate as well as the estate."

Kate thought for a moment. "Check with the teachers and see who her particular friends were," then as an afterthought, "and check whether she was as accident prone when she was with them."

"Yes ma'am."

"Len. What have you got for us on the American college?"

Len conspicuously waved a wodge of papers about as he gave details about the college. Much of it, Kate guessed, came straight from the website. As he finished Kate thanked him and then said, "Right, lunch on me if you can bear the canteen."

Murmurs of appreciation as her team began to put aside paperwork and head for the door. "Go ahead and order, I'll have the veggie option. Len would you spare me a minute?"

Len Goodfellow reluctantly turned back. Kate directed him towards a seat and she sat opposite. "Len can you explain why PC Giles ended up writing the report I had asked you to do?"

Len squirmed. Kate thought he wasn't used to people picking him up on his laziness.

"The American stuff took longer than I thought."

"Len, I gave you that task on Saturday morning. And although your report was detailed I am imaging that most of it came directly from their website. Didn't it?"

A red flush was creeping up his neck and Kate wasn't sure whether this was embarrassment or anger making itself known. Len did not reply.

"Len, in a team it is important that we all carry our fair share of the workload." She reached for the pile of statements from the Blaiseforth staff. "I'd like you to go over these for me and check that we haven't missed anything." Len took them none too graciously and got up to put the papers on his desk.

Kate called after him, "And Len, I want your report for our eight-thirty briefing tomorrow. " Kate thought he was about to object but he merely nodded and stomped out of the room. Kate thought it would be interesting if he turned up for the free lunch or not.

CHAPTER 45

By four the room was stuffy with frustration. No-one seemed to have any new or fresh insights. Kate was at the point of suggesting that everyone needed an early night when Constable Bakir came through the door brimming with news. "Your girl is quite a girl!"

She sat at the small meeting table that Kate directed her to. "Gather round everyone. Time for a break." Whether it was a break from the tedium or break in the case, they didn't care. Her team hastily assembled and looked expectantly at Zara Bakir.

Zara nervously shuffled the papers she'd brought in with her. She wasn't used to being the centre of attention with her colleagues. "Well! I got into the system at the Blaiseforth School quite easily, they need to think about their security. Anyway, almost immediately I found your suspected spyware. Very sophisticated. Basically it is monitoring all aspects but there is something extra in the financial area."

"What kind of extra?"

"That's what I'm not sure of. I think you'll probably need a forensic accountant to look at it. The spyware is sophisticated but the financial gizmo is amazing. As far as I can track it, it seems to be syphoning off small amounts, I mean small, like a few pounds here and there and sending it to an account that is part of the school system but which only the gizmo has access to." Zara Bakir was seriously impressed with what she had found.

"So, somehow Izzy is defrauding the school? Is that what you are saying?" Kate asked.

"I'm really not sure, ma'am. As I say you need an accountant to have a look."

"Okay, thanks Zara, you've given us a lot of food for thought. I still don't know if this ties in with our victim."

"Surely, ma'am," Len contributed, "if the victim had found out that Grey was fleecing the school and threatened to call us in... Wouldn't that be a motive for murder?"

The others around the table seemed to be accepting this scenario.

"That's not all, ma'am." Kate straightened her back. Zara was grinning from ear to ear. "I have this friend in the tech industry and I asked him about what I'd seen of the software and had he seen anything else like it or was it all home grown." She took a deep breath, "He recognised it as a piece of spyware Digiworld patented about eighteen months ago."

Kate interrupted, "Hang on. We think Grey has been using this thing for several years?"

"Oh yes. The amount of stuff it is monitoring goes back about five years."

"So are you saying that this girl got hold of

this way before it was on the market?"

Zara shook her head. "No, she is the creator. Digiwhirled bought it off her. My guess is that she made the spyware and uploaded it into the school system to test it out and get rid of any bugs."

"So would she really care about our victim finding out? If she had money coming in she could just offer to pay back what she borrowed. I'm sure, as headteacher, Miss Betteridge would rather not have such a scandal." Colm mused out loud.

"Good point, Colm."

"Some of this may explain why I'm having problems profiling Izzy Grey's financial records," Alice said. "Firstly I can't find a trust fund that's paying into her account and you did say her fees were being paid from a trust fund set up by her aunt?"

Kate nodded. "It was a great aunt but yes, that's what I was told."

"And," Alice continued, "about two years ago one hundred thousand pounds appeared in her savings account and since then regular quarterly payments of sizeable sums have also been deposited."

"So Izzy Grey is some kind of whizz IT techie who had sold her first creation to an international corporation?" Kate clarified.

"And my friend says there are also rumours that the same creator has a game in development. That would also be worth hundreds of thousands, if it catches on."

"Len can you start a new panel for Izzy Grey – get the details from Zara and Alice."

"Are there any other financial queries?" Colm asked. "With Izzy Grey," he clarified.

"Now we have Zara's info, no. Up until about eighteen months ago there were termly transactions that seemed to show that Blaiseforth Manor paid Izzy and with that money she paid her school fees."

Colm laughed. "So Blaiseforth was paying to have Izzy as a pupil?"

Alice smiled and said, "More or less. I couldn't work it out but with Zara's info it's beginning to make sense. I'll try and get this into some kind of report, ma'am."

"Thanks Alice. Colm, I think you and I need to go and have a chat with Izzy Grey." Despite what she had said Kate remained sat and Colm sat back down again and waited. "No, let's not tip our hand too soon. Colm contact Beth Sandford and ask her to bring Izzy with her," Kate paused. "Say we need to have an official, signed statement but want to let the school settle without our presence."

Colm moved to his own desk and lifted the receiver. Kate checked her watch. She would need to go soon if she was going to eat before meeting with Robin.

CHAPTER 46

Kate had arrived early at the quiet bar in the Golden Lion. The barman smiled in remembrance of her and had asked her if she wanted tea again. Kate was impressed with his memory. Sat in the corner of a settle that gave her a view of the bar's entrance Kate mused on the upcoming meeting. The ping meal lasagne was heavy in her stomach. She tried hard not to fidget or think too much about what Robin wanted. Whatever she imagined Robin would have something else in mind. Better to just wait.

Kate was sipping from her cup when Robin entered. A beaming smile was shot her way and then directed at the barman, who instantly fell under its charm. Robin said something that Kate could not hear but it resulted in a guffaw from the barman and a grin on Robin's face as she walked towards Kate.

She had to admire Robin's style. Tight dark trousers, cut to emphasise Robin's small waist. An equally tight silk top in white topped by a loose sapphire blue open shirt. She prowled, Kate concluded, as she walked across to Kate. Tall and lithe with an undeniable air of confidence. She always looked like she was in her own milieu.
"Kate, thank you for meeting me."

Kate thought she might attempt a hug and

held herself rigidly until Robin sat in the chair opposite. "You asked me to. What do you need to say, Robin?"

Robin took a sip of the amber liquid in her glass. It would be a dry white wine, Kate knew. As she put her glass on the table, Robin cocked a nod at Kate's teapot, "Still tea total!" A bad pun the first time she had used it many years ago.

Robin took another sip. It came in a flash that Robin was nervous. For some reason that made Kate feel more relaxed. They were equals. She was not inferior or subservient to Robin, not any more. "I am in the middle of an important case, Robin, so I can only spare you a half hour."

Robin looked surprised. Kate thought, you're not used to others taking the initiative. It strengthened her resolve that this meeting would not go all Robin's way. Robin took yet another sip and then spoke over the rim of the glass. "I miss you. More than I expected to."

Kate shook her head, "No, Robin. You miss the person you made me be when we were together. That Kate doesn't exist anymore."

"I didn't 'make' you be anyone," Robin remonstrated.

"You did, Robin. You probably didn't even realise that what you were doing was moulding me, but you were."

It was Robin's turn to shake her head. "What did I ever do to make you be someone else?"

"Robin! We've been through this. I don't want

a rehash of our last meeting. It's over. I am not the woman you want in your life."

"But I do."

"So you want someone who will ring and say she's working late and won't make it to the launch party of the latest, whatever?"

"I can cope with that."

"The woman who will no longer accept that the occasional affair is not something to worry about?"

"Kate, I never had affairs."

"So Denise wasn't an affair? Cleo wasn't an affair, Willow, for God sake, what a name. She wasn't an affair?"

Robin twisted the stem of the glass. Turning it round and round on the table. "They were stupid one offs. Only because I was missing you at which ever launch party it was."

Kate snorted. "Robin can you hear yourself? You want me to turn a blind eye to these one night stands because, in part, I'm to blame because I wasn't there?"

"No, that's not what I mean. We were good together and I didn't see it until after you left."

Kate finished the last of her tea and made to leave. "Robin. There's no going back. I like it here in Eashire and I'm doing well in my job. Would you be willing to move here? You could work from home and just have the occasional day in London, couldn't you?"

Kate could tell from the look on Robin's face

that the idea was beyond consideration. "I don't have any hard feelings, Robin, but we are a thing of the past and you are very much a woman who looks to the future."

With that Kate eased herself around the table, waved a farewell to the barman and strode out of the bar. Her chest felt lighter than it had in months, may be even years. She had needed to have that kind of conversation with Robin and had shied away from it, even when they had first broken up. Now it felt good to have kept her cool and told it as it was.

CHAPTER 47

Alice was already at her desk when Kate arrived the next morning. She turned and smiled at Kate and whispered, with one eye on the door, "I don't know what you said to Len yesterday but he was here before me this morning and is brimming with energy!"

"Now that I want to see," said Kate as she hung her jacket on the back of her chair, before Kate went to the murder boards and checked what Len had written about Izzy Grey. Re-reading it now she still could not see this as a motive for murder. Miss Betteridge would have looked for the least public way of dealing with Izzy's theft, if she even knew about it. And they'd found nothing on any of the victim's electronic devices to indicate that she did know.

Colm and Hughes came in together discussing the merits of the local Eashire Rovers as they had made it through to the next stage of the FA cup. "It was amazing, that final goal. Stokes shouldn't have been able to bend it round the post like he did."

"Yeh. I saw it on the slow motion. You won't see that again."

Both men dumped their coats at their desks and made their way to the boards.

Kate was getting ready to recap the

information they had when Len appeared carrying the statements Kate had given him yesterday. Kate could see what Alice meant about the change in him. "Len you look like a man who might have found our golden nugget."

Len smiled like the cat who had got the cream, "I think I might have, boss."

Heads shot up and eyes followed Len to the front of the room. Waving the sheath of papers he began, "The boss asked me to double check the statements we took last Saturday," Kate smiled to herself at the use of 'we' since Len had not been part of that exhausting day. "And I think I've found something." He made a show of looking through the papers until he flourished one in the air.

Putting it in front of him he re-read it. "Marie Meredith, she's what they call a 'Learning Assistant'. On Monday night she had been working late helping some of their year sevens with a geography project, so she didn't leave the school until about six forty-five." Colm rustled his notebook impatiently and Len hurried on.

"She claims that because she was so late leaving, her normal route to the car park was all locked up, so she had to go via the main entrance. She says as she was coming up the corridor she saw one of the lower sixth coming down the stairs that only lead to the landing where Miss Betteridge's rooms are."

"What? At six forty-five?" Kate asked and Len nodded.

"Did she say who it was?" Colm asked.

"No. I did ring her last night and try to jog her memory but all she could say with certainty was that she was a lower sixth girl and that she only saw her side on as she turned away from her at the bottom of the stairs."

"Didn't she challenge the girl?" Kate asked. "I thought those stairs were out of bounds to the girls?"

Len nodded. "I did ask that but she said she thought it must be the girl who was delivering Miss Betteridge her supper so it didn't occur to her to question the girl."

"Well if Izzy's timings are right it can't have been her," said Colm.

"And probably not Kitty because she was waiting for someone to have finished with their text in their common room," concluded Kate.

"We'll need to double check timings with Izzy when she comes in," Colm added.

"Well done, Len. You might just have given us our first real, solid lead. Will you go and interview Ms Meredith again and see if you can jog her memory about any details to give us a handle on who she saw."

Len beamed but made a show of dismissing the praise. "I just happened to notice it in her statement."

CHAPTER 48

Kate had instructed Colm to put Miss Sandford and Izzy in the interview suite that they used for rape victims or children. It was an attractive room, pale but warm yellow walls decorated with pictures of pastoral scenes. The furniture was soft and comfortable and offered chairs and a sofa with a coffee table.

Their agreed strategy was to go in soft. Revisit the night of the murder with particular reference to timings before moving on to the IT issues. Kate was pleased to see that an officer had provided their visitors with a hot drink each and they both looked reasonably relaxed, considering they were in a police station giving a statement.

"Good morning Miss Sandford, Izzy. Thank you for agreeing to come in. We thought it might be kinder for the school if we kept a low profile for a few days."

Miss Sandford nodded her understanding and Izzy looked expectant. Colm took the lead to begin with going over the information Izzy had provided in the first interview. When they got to timings Kate chimed in.

"Izzy, how come you are so sure of the time you left the common room?"

"I checked the clock in the room. I was thinking that the assignment had taken me about an hour-and-a-half and that Kitty was going to be working right up to the close of the common room at eight, probably longer."

"So where does everyone go when the common room closes at eight?"

Miss Sandford interrupted and answered, "The girls go back to their house. There they have the opportunity to relax, watch television, chat, before lights out."

"Okay, thank you. Now, Izzy, while you're here I want to talk to you about your IT skills."

Miss Sandford looked expectant as Kate continued. "When did you plant the spyware in the school IT network?"

Now Miss Sandford looked shocked. She clearly had not expected the police to find anything. She cast a look at Izzy, who wavered between denial and truth.

Izzy then looked directly at Kate, "The system was updated when I was in year seven. I assume someone has been in and seen it? They must have been good not to set off any of my traps."

"You did what? Why?" Miss Sandford was beyond surprised.

Still keeping eye contact with Kate, Izzy explained. "My father was an absolute genius with computers and it was something we did together. By the time I was six I was building my own computers and had the basics of programming under my belt. When he died Dad had just completed the prototype of the spyware you saw. So I saw it as my task to trial it."

Kate nodded her understanding. "So pretending to help Mrs Jessop gave you the opportunity?"

"No!" Izzy was indignant. "I really wanted to help Mrs Jessop. She's nice and treated me as a little girl when everyone else treated me as a problem."

"So you trialled the spyware on the school system? What did you do with the information you acquired?" Colm intervened.

Izzy turned to him. "I wiped it. I wasn't interested in the information itself, just the way the programme worked. I didn't do any harm to the school!" Izzy turned to Miss Sandford for this final sentence.

So far all very reasonable. Kate thought it was time to get down to the crux of the issue. "What about the programme running in the financial system?"

Izzy dropped her eyes and Kate could see colour moving down her neck and when she looked up again her face was red with, what Kate guessed, was embarrassment. At first Izzy tried to call their bluff, "It's just another programme with a financial function."

Kate made a show of tutting. "Not according to our report it's not." Kate flicked through a few pages and allowed Izzy to see they were covered in figures and diagrams, "Do you want to have another go?"

Izzy sighed and seemed to make a decision. "When my parents were killed in their accident the only person who was interested in me was my Great Aunt Amelia, even though she was eighty something. She offered to take me on and sent me here. She said she would rewrite her will so that there would be a trust fund for me if she died before I was eighteen."

"We can't find a trust fund," Colm said.

Izzy sighed again. "I know. She died the first term I was here and hadn't had time to write a new will. Her estate went to a distant cousin who was not going to spend money on me. He said he would pay for the first year and that was it. I told him that if he would continue to officially be my guardian I would spend all the holidays in school and would work out the money for my fees."

"How did he think an eleven year old was going to find money for school fees?" Miss Sandford exclaimed.

The colour, which had been fading during her narrative, flared again. "He never met me so I told him I was sixteen and that I could get work within the school, teaching, to offset my fees."

"And he just accepted that?" Kate asked, shocked by this revelation.

Izzy shrugged, "It was a solution that he didn't have to do anything for. It suited him fine."

"So you embedded another programme to syphon off money from the school that you then used to pay for your fees?"

Miss Sandford groaned and put her head in her hands. "Izzy, why didn't you come and see me. I would have helped."

"I know that now, but back then I'd only just started at the school. I didn't know anyone."

Kate made a show of looking through her papers again as Miss Sandford blew her nose and surreptitiously wiped her eyes. "I notice that about two years ago the financial programme began to work backwards; replacing money a bit at a time."

Izzy nodded. "You probably know that I got a windfall."

"You mean someone paid you for your spyware?" Colm clarified.

"Yes. So I began to replace the money I had used. I couldn't do it all at once and keep it below the radar, so I just reversed the programme."

Colm grinned, "I think it was probably a little more complex than that."

Izzy smiled quietly, "Well, yes. But having my own money means I can repay what I've used and pay properly for my fees."

"Be that as it may. You have defrauded Blaiseforth Manor. Which is a criminal act."

Before Kate could continue Miss Sandford stepped in. "The school will not be pressing charges. This is an oversight. A lack of judgement on Izzy's part which she is now rectifying."

Kate had expected this kind of response and

so let the matter go, for the time being.

"Looking at your funds now, you are truly a wealthy young woman," Kate looked at Izzy, "so why did you enter the Blaiseforth Prize when you obviously don't need the money?"

This time Izzy smiled broadly. "If I hadn't entered everyone would have been wondering why. I was planning, if I was awarded the prize, to step back from it and ask for it to be given to Kitty."

"What about any other entrants?"

Izzy looked mystified. "I didn't know there were any other entrants. I thought only Kitty and I had entered."

Kate caught Colm's eye and gave an imperceptible nod. It was his cue to take Izzy to be fingerprinted whilst Kate continued the interview with Beth Sandford.

CHAPTER 49

Confusion gave way to anxiety as Beth Sandford saw Kate settle in to continue the interview, now with herself. She shook her head slowly, from side to side. "I had no idea! I feel I have let her down."

"Children are remarkably resourceful and that is one remarkable young woman."

Beth nodded. "Can we avoid there being criminal charges? It would be awful to blight such a gifted woman so early on."

"I don't know. I will need to talk with my superiors." Kate put the pile of papers to one side and leant back in the chair. Her shoulders relaxed a little. So far things had gone to plan.

"Izzy seemed surprised that there was more than just the two of them entered for the Blaiseforth Prize, but I was given to understand that there is a third girl?"

"Yes, Chloe Millar."

"So is she very talented like Izzy and Kitty?"

Beth Sandford looked uncomfortable and seemed to be deciding how to answer. Finally she said, "I was surprised when Chloe got two letters of support for her entry. Don't get me wrong, she works very hard and is top of her class in the sciences." Again she looked uncomfortable.

"I sense a 'but'."

"As a scientist myself I would not have said that Chloe was particularly talented, as opposed to very good." She looked at Kate, "Do you understand?"

"So who supported her application?"

"It was her science teacher and her housemistress."

"Is that the normal selection of support?"

"Oh yes."

"So if it had been just Kitty and Izzy who would have won it?"

Beth Sandford sat up straighter, "It is a panel decision."

"I know. But who would your money be on? Just between the two of us."

"I think probably Kitty."

"And if Izzy withdrew and it was between Kitty and Chloe?"

"I would say definitely Kitty." Miss Sandford sighed, "Chloe is an intelligent girl but Kitty is a genius in comparison. She would fulfil the prize's criteria perfectly."

"And just say both Kitty and Izzy were forced to withdraw? Would it automatically go to Chloe?"

"Not necessarily, no. There have been rare years when the prize has not been awarded."

Kate let that answer hang for a moment. Miss Sandford pulled herself up straight and looked Kate in the eye. "Are you saying that you now suspect Chloe Millar of... what? Kitty's accidents?

Elise's death?"

Kate held her hands up in a placatory manner. "I'm not suggesting anything. I'm just trying to gather information. At this stage I can't see any connection with Chloe." What she didn't add was that her sixth sense was buzzing like mad.

Some of the aggression went out of Miss Sandford but she wasn't fully at ease with Kate's stance. "If there is nothing else Inspector I think Izzy and I should be getting back to school."

"Yes of course. We will need to take your fingerprints but purely for elimination purposes."

Kate led Miss Sandford to the IDENT1 office and was not entirely surprised to find Constable Bakir had just happened to be passing and was now deep in conversation with Izzy about how IDENT1 worked.

Having thanked them, Kate left the officer to print Miss Sandford and show them out.

CHAPTER 50

Back in the incident room Kate sat and gazed into the middle distance. No-one seemed a likely candidate for their victim's killer. What was she missing? What else did they need to do? Why was Chloe Millar causing chimes in her mind? Had she heard the name before? They still didn't have enough information. Or the missing piece that would make sense of all the rest.

Coming back to the room she wondered whether they needed to follow up on Chloe. What else needed to be done? Her ruminations were interrupted by the grinning face of Colm. "Boss, I've just had a call from Terry. They've got Phipps in and Terry's boss says we can have a go this afternoon. If we want to go now we can see them having the first round."

"Oh, brilliant. Let's go." Kate grabbed her jacket from the back of her chair. As she left the room she passed Len, "Len, see if you can work your magic again and do a background search on Chloe Millar and her parents, please."

Len almost saluted, "Yes, ma'am. "A girl at the school?"

"Yes. Keep it low key. I just want to know a bit about the family and their finances."

"Who's Chloe Millar?" Colm asked as Kate took the steps down, two at a time.

"Another Blaiseforth Prize entrant," Kate called back over her shoulder."

"And that's important, why?"

"It ties Kitty, Izzy and Chloe together."

"Yes, but how is it connected to the death of our victim?" Colm sounded a little exasperated.

Kate stopped and turned, "I don't know, but something is linking those girls and I'm inclined to believe that somehow it has a bearing on our case." Kate looked at Colm's unsettled face. "Trust me, Colm."

"Yes, boss."

***

An hour later Kate and Colm, along with DC Terry Gilbert were crammed within a dark, and to Kate, testosterone heavy room, watching DCI Wakeford and DC Bell interviewing Gary Phipps. He was the archetype of your estate drugs runner: well-tailored suit with an open necked shirt, short back and sides and a single ear ring. He was casually draped in his chair with one leg resting across the knee of the other. He looked to be in his late twenties and had an air of insouciance about him. Convinced the cops had nothing on him. His solicitor looked less confident. He was a prematurely balding thirty something who looked a tad shabby alongside his fashionable client. He had probably told his client to say 'No comment' but his client had his own ideas.

"He's a cocky git!" said Terry with feeling.

"Have you got anything solid on him?" Kate asked.

"A couple of his runners have been arrested with a range of drugs on them. Some consistent with the vet's robbery. But proving Phipps is running them," Terry shrugged dispiritedly.

Kate thought DCI Wakeford was getting nowhere fast. He must have thought the same because she heard him say, "We will take a break there. Gary can we get you anything? Mr Forbes?"

Both shook their heads as Wakeford and Bell left the room. Seconds later both men added to the testosterone in the viewing room. Terry made the introductions.

"Ah DI Medlar and the ketamine."

"Sir," Kate shook his hand. "Have you found any of it with Phipps?"

"On no! Our Gary wouldn't be anywhere near the stuff. Cocky little bastard. We're going to have a break so do you want to have a go?"

"Yes, please."

"Just be aware we want him for much more than the vet thing."

"Yes, sir."

CHAPTER 51

Feigning that she had no knowledge of Gary's refusal for refreshments Colm and Kate carried four cups of tea into the interview room. It too smelt of sweaty men and of fear and despair. Kate placed a cup on the desk and pushed it across to Gary.

"There you go Mr Phipps. Or may I call you Gary? I wasn't sure how you took it so there's no sugar but it is wet and hot."

Kate sat down as Colm mirrored her action with his spare cup for Mr Forbes. Both men looked surprised to see them and Mr Forbes seemed about to question their presence. Kate held up a hand and explained, "My name is DI Medlar and this is DC Hunter. We have asked if we could have a word with Mr Phipps about an unrelated subject."

Phipps now looked interested, "Well you sure are easier on the eye than Wakeford," he grinned at Kate.

Kate smiled back. "My colleague and I are investigating a murder."

Phipps' face closed down and Forbes began to stutter, "My client has nothing to do with…"

"No. I know. We believe that Mr Phipps may have some knowledge that would help us with our enquiries. We don't think he is directly involved in our case."

Phipps shifted. Despite himself, he was interested with where this pretty little woman was going." Go on then. What do you want to know?"

"How long have you lived on the Camworth estate, Mr Phipps?"

"All my life. Born and bred."

"So would you say you know a lot of people on the estate?"

Phipps looked wary, "Well I probably know a fair few."

"Do you know any girls that go to Blaiseforth Manor?"

"What the posh school?"

Although Kate guessed that Phipps was trying for incredulity she thought he was surprised at the turn of the questions. "Yes. I understand that some of the day girls are known on the estate."

Phipps seemed to be giving this serious thought, "Yeh, now I think about it. I probably do know some."

"Could you think of any names?"

"Nah!" was the instant answer.

Kate didn't pursue this line. She'd come back. "We're specifically looking for someone that was looking for ketamine. An unusual request I would have thought? And you being such a well-known figure on the estate must get to hear most things, eventually?"

Phipps was definitely trying to weigh up what Kate wanted versus his own skin. Kate leaned in, "Look, Gary. I'm not here to trip you up." She bent towards Phipps confidentially, "I just need to know whether someone has been asking about ketamine. I don't even have to know if they found it. Just who was asking."

Phipps rubbed his face with his right hand. "Now you mention it I may have heard about someone asking." Forbes leaned towards Phipps and whispered in his ear but Phipps waved him away.

"I think it was someone who used to know people on the estate. I think she went to school there."

"What the comp?" Kate checked.

"May be, but definitely the little school."

"The primary school?"

"Yeh." He gave it some more thought. "Thinking about it I think she was one of the poshies so she probably did go to the Manor."

"Thanks Gary, that really helps. Do you really not know a name?"

Phipps shook his head.

Colm made a singular contribution, "Any idea of how old this girl might be? You know the one you heard had been asking about the ketamine"

A leer came over Phipps' face. "Old enough for legal sex!"

Kate hoped she kept her face neutral, "So

sixteen, seventeen?"

"Yeh, I think so."

"Thanks for your help, Gary." Kate rose, taking her cup with her.

"Yeh! Just make sure you tell Wakeford that I'm always happy to help when people aren't accusing me of goodness knows what."

Kate nodded and exited with Colm on her heels.

CHAPTER 52

Back in the car Colm asked, "Do you believe him?"

"In the main yes," Kate answered as she clicked her seatbelt in. "I don't want to think about the sex bit. Do you think he was just trying to wind us up?"

"Probably. But with scum like that who can tell? Perhaps that was his price for the ketamine."

Kate was silent for a moment. It was not a pleasing line of thought. She shook her head to deal with the here and now. "Okay. So we now know that someone who went to Camworth Primary and then on to Blaiseforth may have been asking about ketamine."

"I'll get on to that when we get back."

"Check in with Alice. She was looking at Kitty – who went to the primary and now is at Blaiseforth."

Colm sniffed, "You don't think Kitty is the one? Really?"

"To be honest, no. But it should narrow our search down considerably. As I drive give Alice the heads up and see if she can pull some names out."

Colm did as asked and Kate drove back to the station. It was only as she was parking that she realised that she had been on automatic pilot and couldn't remember any of the journey. Instead she had been weighing up everything they knew. It seemed they now had a way forward.

***

The team were all assembled when Kate and Colm arrived back. There was an air of expectancy. Kate knew that feeling. They were getting close. She couldn't see where they were going but they were certainly travelling towards it.

"Okay everyone. Take a seat. What has today brought us?"

They all sat around the table with sheaves of paper in front of them. Once again Len was brimming over with enthusiasm. This time Kate thought he should wait, so she began. "Well, Colm and I have had an interesting conversation with a Mr Gary Phipps, drug dealer of this parish. Of course he admits nothing. However, he did say that he 'heard'," Kate mimed the quote marks, "that a young woman was asking about ketamine."

Murmurs greeted this news. "And," Kate continued, "she probably went to the estate primary and then on to Blaiseforth. So Alice, what have you got for us?"

Alice calmly handed out a single sheet of paper to each of them. "With Colm's information about the primary and Blaiseforth link I was able to narrow the names down, in Kitty's year group, to just three names, at the top of your paper."

Kate read, Kitty Hardcastle, Denise Church and Chloe Millar.

Alice continued, "If you look at the next list of names those are the girls from the years above and below Kitty."

Kate read again. There were only five names and none stood out. Kate went back to the first three names. "Chloe Millar's name seems to have cropped up a couple of times before. What do you have on the Millars, Len?"

Self-importantly Len began, "Chloe Millar only daughter of Megan and Christopher Millar," Kate's sixth sense was twitching. Where had she heard those names in combination before? "Apparently there was a boy," Len continued but he died as a few months old, Sudden Infant Death Syndrome according to the death certificate. Whatever it was it broke the wife and there was concern that she couldn't look after her daughter, who was just eleven, with the husband working away on construction sites."

Len gave a dramatic pause before delivering the final gem, "With the help of Megan's parents, Jack and Audrey Newton, the family paid for Chloe to attend Blaiseforth Manor as a boarder."

Colm spluttered into life, "He didn't tell us his grand-daughter was at the same school that his new girlfriend was head of."

Kate doodled on Alice's list, "No, indeed. He didn't. I think Mr Newton needs another visit."

"Before you go, ma'am," Len continued holding up his notebook. "I went and interviewed Marie Meredith, the Learning Support Assistant. She couldn't really add very much. I tried to get her to close her eyes and rethink the event. The best she could come up with was," he consulted his book again, "definitely a lower sixth girl. Probably about five foot five and shoulder length dark hair."

"Not much to go on," Colm muttered, "It probably covers about half the girls there."

"I don't know," mused Kate. "It will weed out fair and red heads, long hair and short. At least it's cutting the numbers down." Kate turned back to Len, "Thanks Len."

"Right, Colm, you're with me. Mr Newton needs another visit."

CHAPTER 53

"What reason could he have for killing her? Do you think it is all connected?" Colm threw out comments as Kate negotiated the roads. Colm continued to hypothesise out loud. "How did he get into the school without being noticed?" He shook his head and then cried out, "You don't think he got his grand-daughter to do the killing? Oh surely not."

Kate tuned Colm out. Her brain was also racing through possible scenarios. And the more she thought about it the more the dread filled her stomach. Did they really have a teenage killer? And, the golden question, what was her motive? As they turned onto Newton's estate Kate cut across Colm's monologue. "We're going to focus on his grand-daughter. Get him chatting about her and then move to the financial situation. At this stage we can't rule him in or out."

Drawing up outside Newton's house, Kate was pleased to see that the car was in place and the lights on. It was just after six and she had wondered whether they would have to wait for him to return from seeing his wife.

Walking up to the house, Kate touched the car bonnet as she passed. It was still warm. He clearly hadn't been in long. Colm tapped firmly on the door. Jack Newton took his time opening it and was surprised to see them. "Hello. Do come in. I'm just cooking my tea."

They both entered and stood in the hall. The smell of bacon cooking was strong in the air. "Go in," Jack flapped a hand in the direction of the living room, "I'll just go and turn everything off."

Once in the living room Kate went to the latest photograph of Chloe Millar. In it she looked, may be early teens. Jack had said before that it was four or five years old. The face that looked back at her was wary. Was it her imagination but did Chloe look like a girl with hidden depths? Not all of them pleasant?

Jack Newton returned. "Ah, still admiring Chloe?"

Kate smiled, "I hadn't realised that she was a pupil at Blaiseforth Manor. What year is she?"

"She's just done her GCSEs. Got all As or A*s. Bright button that one. She wants to go on to university but that's an expensive business now, isn't it? All that debt they run up."

"Did Miss Betteridge realise that Chloe was your grand-daughter?"

"Oh yes. I told her from the off. She said it would make no difference to the way she dealt with Chloe, should their paths cross. And I believed her."

"Does Chloe know about your relationship with Miss Betteridge?"

Jack Newton looked confused. "I don't know. I don't think so. What is this all about,

Inspector?"

Kate feigned innocence, "We're just checking all the connections with Miss Betteridge. This was one we came across and wanted to clarify."

Jack Newton did not look convinced. "Chloe is an excellent pupil and is a credit to all of us, considering what she's been through."

Kate looked enquiring and Jack got up from his chair and went to the more recent photographs. He picked up the one of the baby that was not Chloe. He handed it to Kate, "That is Daniel, my grandson. He died when he was five months, one week and three days old. They called it SIDS. You know Sudden Infant Death Syndrome."

Kate looked at the photograph. It looked like so many baby photographs she had seen but she could feel Jack's pain. "I'm sorry for your loss. How long ago was this?"

"Almost seven years ago. It devastated all of us but was particularly hard on my daughter. She went to pieces. A breakdown." His eyes glazed over. "She couldn't look after herself, let alone care for Chloe, and Christopher's job takes him all over the country so my wife and I made a decision. We sold our old house and invested it for Chloe's school fees. We paid for her to be a boarder to give Megan a chance to get back on her feet."

"That was very generous of you. I would have thought it was the last thing you planned to do with your retirement," Kate said.

"Yes, well, the best laid plans," Jack sighed.

"Are you still paying for Chloe's fees?" Kate was thinking this would be a tall order now with his wife in The Orchards. It was a lovely place but Kate was sure it wouldn't be cheap.

Jack shook his head regretfully, "No. Audrey's fees are too large. Megan and Chris sold their home and moved to the Camworth estate and are using the proceeds to allow Chloe to finish her time at the school as a day girl."

Kate's radar prickled. "So your daughter lives quite close by?"

Jack nodded and Kate continued, "I'd assumed that if you went to stay with her that she lived away from the area."

Jack smiled. "No, It's not far but it is company and it is a change of routine and a change of the four walls."

"Could we have her address, please?"

Jack readily gave it and Colm noted it down. Kate glanced at Colm to see if he had anything to ask. Noticing he closed his notebook, they both got up. "Sorry to have taken up your time again, Mr Newton. I hope your tea has survived the hiatus."

He gave a false chuckle. "Oh it'll be fine. I'm no great shakes as a cook but at least I've stopped burning stuff."

CHAPTER 54

"Megan and Chloe Millar?"

"Oh yes. But not now. I don't think he deliberately misled us but we seem to have uncovered an awful lot that would have been useful to know earlier."

"What if he warns them that we're coming to visit?"

"That's one of the reasons why we're going to leave it for tonight. They will either stew that we've not come or relax. Either way they will be unsure."

Kate slipped into gear and continued, "If Chloe is living on Camworth she has easy access to Gary Phipps and his products."

"Yeh, but if she's not a boarder how can she have been in the school that evening? Wouldn't she have been noticed?"

"Possibly, but it's an enormous place. How easy would it be to find a quiet place to hole up in?"

"So how did she explain her absence to the parents? Was she out all night or did she slip out and back in again when she had done the deed?" Colm's tone was a little ironic.

"I don't know, Colm. But she's seventeen. How easy would it be to say you were stopping over with a friend? Or stopping over to do some extra work? If her parents are anything like Jack they think the sun shines out of her backside. Are they going to question too closely?"

"But that's the other point. Everyone says she is an excellent pupil. What would make her kill someone?"

"Yes, everyone has said she's a good pupil but has anyone said she's a good person? A kind person?"

Colm shrugged. "It still seems a bit far-fetched that a pupil killed their Head. What's the motive?"

"I don't know but I'll bet you a posh dinner on me that it all ties back to the Blaiseforth Prize. Which means Bart was right – follow the money. Tomorrow I want to interview the head of science and Chloe's housemistress. Find out why they supported her application."

"But what about Megan? And Chloe herself?"

"I want to gather as much info as we can before we go near them. I don't want to let Chloe know we are getting close."

"So you really think she did it?"

Kate hesitated but then said, "Yes. I don't know why and how she managed to carry it out without being seen, but yes, I think she did it."

Colm gave a silent whistle. "Are you going to tell Bart all this?"

Kate glanced at Colm. He had always been a good colleague but it was clear that he was finding her conclusions hard to deal with. Would he go to Bart behind her back? Tell him she was obsessed with the Blaiseforth Prize and the involvement of the girls. "I will tell Bart but after we have done the initial interviews. We will at some point need a search warrant for their house."

Colm nodded. "Sure, boss."

CHAPTER 55

The following morning Kate brought her team up to date with their visit to Jack Newton the night before and future actions. There was still that buzz in the air. They all sensed they were reaching a critical point. Kate just hoped she was right about the ending. Her first case as the senior investigating officer. She mustn't foul this up. She had spent all night second guessing herself. At some points she seemed convinced that it all led to Chloe Millar but then self-doubt and its friend anxiety stepped in and knocked her ideas down like so many wooden building blocks.

Now in front of her team she hoped she projected confidence and surety. "Alice, would you look into the death of a Daniel Millar, a baby? About five years ago. Were we involved? Was there any question over the verdict of SIDS as the cause of death?"

Alice nodded as she made notes about the search. Kate then turned to Sergeant Hughes, "Can you make a start on drawing up a request for a warrant of Chloe Millar's home and any storage space; a locker, that type of thing, at the school? Don't action it until I give the word. I will need to talk it through with Bart."

Hughes also nodded as he made notes. Kate

turned to look for Len. "No Len?" she asked the room at large.

Alice answered, "He said he had an idea and was going back to the school to talk again with the assistant.

"Okay. We'll probably come across him when we get there. Thanks everyone. I think we're close to the end."

Murmurs greeted this and the positive vibe heightened.

"Come on then, Colm. Let's go and find out why those two teachers supported Chloe's application."

***

Colm was detailed off to find out from Mrs Jessop where they could find Mrs Piper and Miss Blackwell. The two teachers who had supported Chloe Millar's Blaiseforth Prize application. Kate made her way to the interview room where she found Len gazing at a set of portrait photographs on one of the tables. "Morning ma'am. I just contacted the station and they said you were on your way so I waited for you."

"Morning Len," Kate said as she made her way over to him and stood alongside and looked at four school photographs of four girls or young women. There was a similarity between the four; all of them with the slightly soft features that hadn't yet settled for their adult look. All with the attempt at rule breaking with their mascara and probably a dash of rouge. Only their hair made some differentiation but even here it was limited. They were all a darker shade of brown and worn loose, only the length and in one a slight wave to the flow made a difference.

Len smiled, "I knew from my lads that the school would have an annual photo of the girls so I got Mrs Meredith to take a look. These were all taken at the end of year eleven so they're about eight months out of date. I told her not to worry too much about the hair. And she came up with these four."

"Good thinking, Len." Kate moved the photos around, "I can see her problem, these all have a similarity."

"Umm. I did wonder whether I should have got her to look at the year groups either side but she was quite adamant that it was a lower sixth girl."

Kate bent and looked more closely at each portrait. She thought she knew which one was Chloe Millar. There was something about the set of her face. May be the look in the eyes. Something contained.

Len tapped one of the photos, "That's our girl, Chloe Millar. Mrs Jessop confirmed that she wears her hair shorter now."

It was the one Kate had identified. In this photo the girl had long hair, brushed back over her shoulders. "Thanks, Len. I'll keep these for now."

At that moment Colm came in carrying two cups of tea, "Courtesy of Mrs Jessop. Sorry Len I didn't realise you were in here."

"No problem. I'm off." He almost saluted as he left.

Colm smiled. "I don't know what you've done with the old Len Goodfellow but I like this new one."

Kate also smiled. "I think it's the first time he has had the thrill of the chase and some success." She flicked the photos across to Colm. "One of these is our girl. Care to pick?"

Colm put the two teas down and came and peered over the portraits. For several minutes he stared and picked up and put down each slip of paper and finally said, "I don't know how old these are because it doesn't quite fit the description but there's something about this one that doesn't feel right." He too had picked out Chloe Millar.

"What about our two teachers?"

Mrs Jessop has arranged for someone to fetch Mrs Piper, apparently she's free at the moment and then she will talk to Miss Sandford about getting cover for Miss Blackwell for the next lesson."

"Good."

CHAPTER 56

Kate was shuffling through the photographs when there was a firm knock on the meeting room door and a middle aged woman wearing a beaming smile put her head round the door, "Inspector Medlar?"

"Yes, come in. Mrs Piper?" Mrs Piper nodded in acknowledgement, "This is my colleague DC Hunter."

"Pleased to meet you." Mrs Piper shook each of them by the hand before sitting in a seat opposite where Colm and Kate were sat. "I'm assuming this is about poor Elise, but I really don't know how I can help."

"At the moment we're just trying to understand the school structure," Kate lied. "I understand you're a housemistress?"

"Yes. I am. For Mary Anne Evans House."

She waited a fraction and was about to continue when Colm supplied, "As opposed to George Elliott?"

Mrs Piper beamed, "Well done. Most people know George Elliott was a pseudonym for a woman but rarely remember her real name. This is our attempt to change that, a little."

Put me in that category, Kate thought before asking, "Sorry to be so ignorant but what does a housemistress do?"

Another beam, "Most people would understand it better as a pastoral role. For the little ones making sure they're not too homesick; not worrying about work; that they're happy and content. That sort of thing."

"What about the older girls?"

"Well similar really but hopefully by then I've developed a more personal relationship with them so that they see me as someone they may confide in."

"So you're responsible for all years in your house?" Kate clarified.

"Yes, but each year has an assistant mistress. In a normal school it's a bit like having a head of year and then tutors. Just in my case we have vertical groups not horizontal."

"What about the day girls?" Colm interceded.

"I don't have quite so much contact but the assistant mistress for their year would."

"I understand you wrote a supporting letter for Chloe Millar for the Blaiseforth Prize but she's a day girl."

Mrs Piper looked surprised at the change of tact but she followed willingly. "Yes, but Chloe had been a boarder so I know her quite well. It has been a tough few years for her."

"Is that why you wrote the letter?"

"Sorry, I'm not sure I understand what you're asking."

"Do you think Chloe is good enough to be considered for the prize or did you write it because she's had a hard time?"

"I... er..."

Colm leant forward confidentially, "Mrs Piper, we need an honest answer to that question. We promise that whatever is said in here will not go any further, but we do need an honest answer." He smiled in the way only Colm could.

Mrs Piper fidgeted in her chair. She looked down at her hands. Kate was sure calculations were being made. Finally she looked up.

"I was surprised to be asked to write a supporting letter. Chloe is a hard worker but not what this school would call outstanding."

"So why didn't you gently turn Chloe down?"

Mrs Piper looked directly at Kate, "Because it was Miss Betteridge who asked me to write it." Having revealed that nugget she relaxed once more. "She said that Chloe had spoken to her about it and, given the circumstances of the last few years, it would be a kindness to let her think that she would be considered."

There was silence for a few seconds and then Kate spoke, "Forgive me but that doesn't sound like the sort of thing the Miss Betteridge we have come to know, would do."

Mrs Piper savoured that comment and then slowly nodded. "Yes. I have to admit I was surprised by her interference but I took it at face value and wrote the letter."

"Did Chloe herself come and ask you to write

to support her application?" Colm asked.

"She did, but I think she already knew I had been asked. There was a sort of expectation that the answer would be yes."

"So you think that Miss Betteridge had already spoken with Chloe?"

"That was my assumption, yes."

"What do you think of Chloe? Not as a pupil here but as a human being?"

Now there was a distinct pause, "I'm not sure what you mean?"

"Well, everything we've been told about Chloe is that she is good at science; that she's a hard worker; that she's had a tough time. But nothing about what she is like as a person."

"Oh, I see. Well..." Again a pause. Mrs Piper was clearly finding it difficult to find the right words to describe Chloe Millar. "She's very self-contained. Doesn't mix easily. And this has become more pronounced with the problems a few years ago."

"These 'problems' are they the family's money problems and her becoming a day girl rather than a boarder?"

Mrs Piper nodded. "She didn't have a friendship circle and so it was even more difficult for her when she left and then came back."

So Chloe has been here for almost six years, with this hiatus, and doesn't have a friendship group?" Colm couldn't keep the incredulity out of his voice.

Mrs Piper bristled slightly, "We did what we could but she is just not a mixer. She's polite and interacts with the other girls, but it's all on a superficial level."

Kate waited in case there was any more Mrs Piper wanted to add and then rose and put out a hand to shake Mrs Piper's. "Thank you for your honesty. You have helped a great deal."

Mrs Piper rose and reciprocated the handshake with a raised eyebrow. Colm walked her to the door with a final, "Thank you Mrs Piper."

CHAPTER 57

As soon as the door was closed Colm asked, "What do you think – our victim trying to favour her boyfriend's grand-daughter or a bit of blackmail?" Back at the table he took out the photo of Chloe Millar. "I think blackmail."

Kate grimly nodded. "Yes. I can't see the woman we've been told about interfering with the system, or cooking the books. But what did Chloe have as blackmail material?"

"I don't know, something along the lines of 'I'll tell the trustees you're having an affair with my granddad'?"

Any further discussion was curtailed by the arrival of Miss Blackwell. A small woman who looked like she'd borrowed her mother's lab coat which licked at her ankles.

"Ah, Miss Blackwell," Kate welcomed her in and directed her to a seat.

"Call me Greta. I have enough 'Miss Blackwell' all day."

"Thank you, Greta." Kate thought she would begin with Colm's spiel about confidentiality and honesty.

Greta nodded, "Ask away. I'll try to be honest." There was a twinkle in her eye which Kate warmed to.

"Mrs Piper was telling us about the

Blaiseforth Prize," Kate lied again. This was becoming a habit! "It must be quite an honour for the department represented as well as the girl chosen?"

"Oh yes. We're always on the lookout for that extra spark of talent."

"Have the sciences had many winners?" Colm asked.

Greta's face took a down turn. "Unfortunately, not for more than a decade. Even in a girls' school the sciences can be a hard sell. We do have several talented biologists in the lower school at the moment so I am busy nurturing them." She twinkled again.

"What about Chloe Millar?"

"Ah." The twinkle disappeared. "Chloe. You obviously know I have written in support of her application." She didn't wait for a response. "I have to admit it went against my better judgement but Elise herself came and asked me to do so."

"What reason did she give for her interference?"

"She said that she had spoken with the girl who had her heart set on being able to apply and with all that unpleasantness a couple of years ago it seemed a small thing to do."

"What was this 'unpleasantness'?"

"As far as I understand it and from the malicious comments of some of the girls, Chloe's boarding fees were, at least in part, paid by her grandparents."

Kate nodded without intimating that she already knew this information.

"Then, when her grandmother had to go into care they could no longer afford to do so. Chloe was taken out of school and we thought that we'd not see her again. Then she came back as a day girl. I believe her parents sold their house and moved to the Camworth estate. Chloe got a lot of stick from some of the girls."

"Anyone in particular?"

"I'm not sure of names but I believe, and here I have to admit that this is staffroom gossip, that Izzy and Kitty intervened. Izzy suggested that some of them might find they would have problems with their electronic devices." The twinkle was back. "I know I shouldn't applaud such threats but everyone knows that Izzy is a whizz with computers and the like. They all knew she could carry out her threat."

"Were Izzy and Kitty particular friends of Chloe's?"

"I don't think so but the pair of them, for different reasons, know what it's like to be on the edge. Not quite part of the group. I think their good nature was their motive."

"So who are Chloe's friends and why didn't they step in when the bullying started?"

Greta hesitated before replying. "Chloe is a loner. Even in class where lab buddies are normal Chloe prefers to work alone and, I'm sorry to say, if she is paired up with anyone they are not comfortable with her. In recent years I have allowed Chloe to work by herself."

"Do you think Chloe has a chance of winning the prize?"

"Honestly, no. She works hard but she doesn't have that flair."

"How about if Kitty or Izzy withdrew their application?"

Greta shook her head. "I'm sorry to say, the only way she would win it would be if both Izzy and Kitty withdrew and even then the panel might not award it."

Kate queried, "So they don't have to award the prize?"

"I'm not one hundred per cent certain but I think there have been three years when the prize was not awarded."

"Thank you, Greta. You have been very helpful. We'll let you get back to your class."

Greta groaned as she stood and stepped towards the door, "The trials and tribulations of zygotes with year seven."

CHAPTER 58

"I think it's time we visited Mrs Millar."

"What about Chloe?"

"No, she can wait. I want to talk to her mother and perhaps get a look in Chloe's room."

Kate was heading for the exit doors of the foyer when she stopped abruptly, causing Colm to sidestep to avoid her. "What's the matter?"

"Just want to check something with Beth Sandford before we go." Kate turned and headed for the Head's office. She knocked and waited until she heard Beth Sandford's permission to enter.

The Head's eyebrows rose.

"Good morning Inspector, I was aware you were in, talking to Mrs Piper and Miss Blackwell?"

Kate ignored the question in the comment. "Yes, thank you. I just wanted to clarify a couple of things about the Blaiseforth Prize with you."

Beth Sandford reluctantly put her pen down and leaned back. Her body language showed impatience but she was trying to mask it.

"How much is the prize worth? I'm assuming it is a large amount?"

"Yes. It is a touch under fifty thousand pounds. Every ten years the trustees recalculate the original sum in terms of modern inflation."

"Thank you. I understand that a panel of

teachers decide the winner?"

Beth Sandford nodded and then said, "Generally it is the Head, myself, the four house mistresses and the heads of the subjects being represented by the applicants."

"So this year there would have been nine members of the panel? Would that mean that Miss Betteridge would have had the casting vote?"

Miss Sandford became more alert, "Ordinarily, yes but actually just after Christmas, Elise said that this year she would not sit on the panel and would leave the casting vote to me."

"Why was that?"

Beth Sandford shook her head, "She said she had a fondness for all three applicants and wasn't sure she could be impartial! Also that she was going to be busy with the new building project."

"Did you believe her?"

Beth Sandford paused. "To be honest, no," she finally offered. "Elise had a very strong moral compass and I cannot imagine her allowing emotions to cloud her judgement. Maybe the building work was more of a reason but I can't see her letting it get in the way."

"Thank you. I'm sorry we had to interrupt your day again."

Kate turned to leave and was halted by a request, "You will let me know when you have your suspect, won't you?"

Kate turned back. "When we are sure. Yes. I will personally let you know."

***

Back in the car Kate asked, "What does that conversation tell us, Colm?"

Colm blew out his cheeks and replayed the information they had gathered that morning. "If Chloe was blackmailing our victim in the hope of getting the Blaiseforth money she was stymied by her withdrawing from the selection panel. But is that motive enough for murder?"

Kate rubbed her eyes, "I'm not sure but let's play this out. If you were desperate to win the money how would you try to influence the panel?"

"Well she couldn't kill off all the panel members so…" Colm tailed off as his mind began its own jigsaw. "But she might try and do something to get rid of or discredit her rivals." No sooner had he said it then Colm argued against it. "No! That's ridiculous."

"It may explain Kitty's accidents."

Silence filled the car until Colm said, "Okay *if* we accept that, how does she get rid of Izzy? Because she would need to if she wanted to be seriously considered for the money. And Greta said they have had years when it's not been awarded."

"She may have thought that there was a shadow over Izzy already because she took the tray in to our victim."

"True, but we'd need some kind of evidence to take that further."

Kate tapped her forefinger on her lips. "I would guess that Chloe's next move would be to plant evidence in Izzy's room."

"But how would she get us to the stage where we would search the room?"

"Umm. Not sure. But I wonder if we should pre-empt her or wait and see how she does it?"

"You're really sure that Chloe Millar is behind all this?" Colm's doubts marred his face.

"Yes, I do. Now we need to find the evidence."

Transcript Audio Log 1min 10secs

No-one knows how to treat Izzy now. She had to go to the police station and make a statement but she was gone a long time. Most of the girls think it's just because she took in the supper tray and more than one has said how glad she is that she hadn't offered to help Kitty out. Others are looking sideways at Izzy. They wonder if there is more to it.

Whilst Izzy was at the station I put my plan into action. Getting into her room was easier than I had expected. I'd found a bunch of keys in the stockroom and so far hadn't found a door that any of them fitted but with a bit of jiggling and pushing I managed to get Izzy's lock to jump.

Her room was just like mine was when I was a boarder. No really good places to hide anything. But I didn't want to make it too difficult or the plods may not find it. In the end I opted for the finger of a pair of gloves and hid them in the back of the bottom drawer. I made sure that the phial was wiped clean and that anything I may have touched was wiped down.

Let Izzy talk her way out of this one. Now all I have to do is get someone to ring the station. I'll talk to Gary.

CHAPTER 59

Just as Kate drew away from the school her phone rang. Pulling over in the drive she answered it. A smile spread across her face at the information supplied. "Thanks Alice. That is great. Yes DC Hunter and I will act on that now."

She put her phone away and reversed back into the parking space they'd just left. Colm's face asked the question and Kate answered, "An anonymous tip off has just come into the station. The girl who may have been asking about the ketamine was possibly called Izzy." She stared at Colm who shook his head in wonder.

"Our reason to search!" He finally said. "Any idea who the tip off was from?"

"Alice said it came through on the front desk and the desk Sergeant just made a note of the info and the caller rang off before he could be asked anything else."

"He? Gary Phipps?"

"Or one of his employees." Kate got out of the car. "Come on then. Let's go and upset Miss Sandford, again."

And upset she was, "You want to search Izzy's room? What on earth are you thinking?"

Kate tried to placate, "I'm really sorry but we have to act on information we receive. If you wish we can wait and have an official warrant drawn up."

Beth Sandford ran her fingers through her smooth bob causing static hairs to halo her head. "I want to give Izzy the choice. It's up to her."

Izzy was sent for and arrived within five minutes. Five very long minutes as Beth Sandford glared her disapproval and all attempts at polite conversation failed. Izzy looked wide-eyed at each of the adults in the room. Some of her earlier poise was gone. The whole school now whispered that Miss Betteridge had been murdered.

Kate tried to control the moment, "Izzy come and take a seat." She directed Izzy to one of the sofas. As she did this Beth Sandford came from behind her desk and sat next to Izzy. She took charge of the conversation. "Izzy, the police would like to search your room. You have every right to refuse permission."

"But why? Why do they want to search it?" She looked directly at Kate.

Kate did not want to reveal the tip off, especially as she thought it was a set up and so said, "It's part of our procedure. You took the tray into Miss Betteridge and so we have to follow up on that."

Izzy shook her head in bewilderment. "I don't have anything to hide so yes you can search it."

"You don't have to," Miss Sandford repeated.

"No. I'm happy for them to search now. If I

refuse it makes me look like I have something to hide," she had been addressing Miss Sandford but now turned to Kate. "You have my permission to search my dorm and my locker. Shall I show you to them?"

"Thank you, Izzy. We really appreciate your cooperation."

Izzy showed them out of the oldest part of the school, across the quad to, what looked to Kate like a small modern manor house. Izzy led them to her dorm; a small room on the top floor.

Kate and Colm put on forensic gloves and footwear and followed Izzy in. The room had a single bed, a wardrobe and a chest of drawers on one side; a desk and chair on the other and a door which, on checking led to a bathroom.

Izzy and Beth Sandford hovered in the doorway. "Shall I go away, wait outside? What do you want me to do?" asked Izzy.

Kate pointed to the desk chair, "Sit there and watch. Make sure that we are doing this right. Miss Sandford, are you happy to watch from the door?"

Beth Sandford nodded.

Reluctantly Izzy sat and watched as Kate went through her chest of drawers and Colm through her wardrobe. Kate had hoped that if Izzy saw that it was her going through her underwear she wouldn't feel as uncomfortable as if it was Colm. The final drawer in the chest was more an odds and sods kind of place. Spare notebooks, printing paper, an old teddy, a scarf and pair of gloves. It was in the gloves that Kate found their evidence; a small glass phial, clearly labelled as ketamine.

Kate held it up for Izzy to see. "She went white and began to shake, "I... I... I've never seen that before. Honestly I don't know what it is or where it's come from."

Kate believed her. Izzy was an intelligent young woman; she would have found a far more inventive hiding place but she had to act on the find. Carefully she labelled an evidence bag, placed the phial in it and sealed it up. "We'll have to analyse this. In the meantime I am going to trust that you will stay in school. I am making Miss Sandford responsible for your presence here. Do you understand?"

Izzy nodded and Beth Sandford came into the room and put a comforting arm around Izzy's shoulders. "I am absolutely convinced that your evidence has been planted."

Kate wondered if Beth Sandford would take that comment to its logical conclusion. Who could have planted it?

Kate and Colm made a show of continuing to search Izzy's room but she knew they had found what they'd been intended to find. At the end of the hour or so Kate asked if Beth Sandford could find another room for Izzy to occupy until forensics had done a sweep. In the meantime Kate would lock the door and retain the key. Colm went back to the car and placed the obligatory police tape across the door in a z shape.

Leaving Izzy in Beth Sandford's care, they left the school.

CHAPTER 60

Kate got Colm to drive back to the station while she rang Mike.

"Hi, Mike. Kate Medlar. I'm going to be dropping off evidence for analysis. Yes a glass phial, possibly one of our missing ketamine phials. Yes. I also need a small team back to Blaiseforth Manor to go over one of the girl's rooms. Yes. But wait until I arrive as I have the key to the room, although we have also sealed it. Yes. About twenty minutes." She hung up and sat back in her car seat. Had they at last got a handle on this? Was it really all about the Blaiseforth Prize?

Colm broke into her meditation. "You seem to be right."

"Umm. I think when we're back at the station I need to run this past Bart. This," she held up the evidence bag with the phial, "is our first solid evidence and, at the moment, is pointing away from our hypothesis."

"Mike's team might come up with some fingerprints."

"May be. Chloe thinks she's directing this investigation so she may have been careless when planting the evidence but…" she left the sentence unfinished. Chloe had proved to be an intelligent adversary. Would she slip up in the last stretch?

***

Back at the station Kate dropped both the evidence and the key to Mike, whose team was ready to go. In the incident room Alice approached Kate at her desk. "Boss, I looked into the death of Millar's son and there didn't appear to be anything amiss and other than an original attendance the force was not involved. However, the attending officer is now a DI in another force and I took the liberty of contacting him for a chat." She opened her notebook. "PC Gareth Staines attended the Millar's family home at about six-thirty in the morning following an incoherent 999 call. He said he remembers it well because the mother was hysterical, the father was distraught but the young girl, Chloe, was calm and apparently unaffected by the drama around her."

Kate interrupted, "How old was Chloe at the time?"

"Eleven. She's at the older end of her year group."

"So she was old enough to know what had happened," Kate mused. "Did PC Staines have any further thoughts about the case?"

"Not at the time, no. But he said on the phone, that every so often, when he looks back at it, her behaviour did strike him as odd."

"Did he think Chloe was involved?"

"I did ask him that and he wasn't keen to make a decision. He just said it struck him as odd but perhaps that was the way she responded to shock."

"The coroner clearly had no doubts."

"No. The post-mortem did not show any signs of deliberate suffocation and so SIDS was given as the cause of death."

"Thanks, Alice. Can you add that to Chloe's column on the board, please? Once you're done I'll get Colm to add the information from our interviews this morning. Would you also let the team know that a piece of evidence was found in Izzy's room, which is with forensics at the moment."

Alice's face fell. "Oh. That's a shame. Zara really liked her. Said she was one of the most talented programmers she's ever had a chat with."

"Don't count her in, entirely. I'm wondering if our tip-off is part of a deliberate attempt at misdirection."

Alice's face lifted. "That's very cunning. So you think someone planted the evidence, boss?"

Kate nodded, "I think that's a strong possibility."

***

Kate's interview with DCI Bartholomew was much longer and more in depth than she had anticipated. Having laid out their activities and then her conclusions Bart then took her through it all again. Where there were gaps he asked Kate how she would fill them. Where it was unclear he asked Kate to clarify. Eventually he sat back and smoothed back his hair from his face with both hands. "Okay, Kate. I can see your reasoning, but you don't have one iota of evidence that leads to Chloe Millar. In fact you have evidence that leads to someone else entirely."

Kate went to answer but he held a hand up to stop her. "What do you hope to find by searching Chloe's home and locker? A diary telling all?"

"We might find the other phials."

"If Chloe is as cute as you say then she will have already got rid. And even if you do find it she could claim it was planted, just like Izzy's was."

"But we do have to search, sir."

"I agree but as I see it you are only going to prove this if you get a confession. So what makes Chloe tick? How are you going to either gain her trust or get under her skin?"

Kate sat and thought. Bart was right. "We need to find out as much as we can about Chloe before we go and interview her parents and Chloe herself, don't we?"

Bart nodded. "I am happy to authorise the

search request but get some more ammunition first."

Kate was already planning as she left Bart's office. She wanted to move quickly. Time to set her team off in lots of different directions.

CHAPTER 61

Fifteen minutes later Kate had gathered her team together. Briefly she and Colm gave their feedback about their victim's manipulations behind Chloe's application for the Blaiseforth Prize and Alice relayed the possible concern the attending officer had at the death of Chloe's brother.

"Right, before we go in and challenge Chloe we need as much information as possible about her. What makes her tick? What are her likes and dislikes? Does she have friends? Everything we can possibly track down."

Kate looked around the table. Only Sergeant Hughes was not looking at her as he updated the murder book. "Colm I want you to visit The Orchard, the home where Chloe's grandmother, Audrey Newton is being cared for. According to Miss Hazel the last time Chloe visited, Audrey was scared to death of her and screamed blue murder. Try to find out what happened and whether it's happened to anyone else."

"Yes, boss." Colm noted the details down.

"Len, I want you to track down Chloe's teachers from the primary school and the Millar's neighbours before they moved to Camworth. What was Chloe like? How did she get on with others? You know the sort of thing."

"Yes, boss."

"Alice you are coming with me, back to the school. I want to interview some of the girls and I think they may respond to a younger figure. Do you have civvies with you?"

"Yes."

"Right, go and change." Alice got to her feet hurriedly and left the room.

"If there's nothing else?" No-one said a word. "Okay. We'll meet back here at five."

"Should we synchronise watches, boss?" Colm asked, grinning.

Kate grinned back. "No, but don't be late."

Whilst waiting for Alice's return, Kate rang Beth Sandford. Their luck was in, Kate thought, when she heard that Wednesday was a half day, a little like a Saturday but the girls were mainly in study groups, especially the lower sixth.

"There are specific girls I'd like to talk with so could I have a list of the girls in each group, please?" Kate looked up as Alice returned in casually cut trousers and a sweatshirt. Perfect, thought Kate. "We will be with you within half-an-hour. Thank you." Kate rang off.

"That woman will deserve a bunch of flowers by the time this is over!"

Alice grinned.

"Ready, boss."

Beth Sandford came out of her office with the lists Kate had requested. As she handed them over Kate asked, "How's Izzy doing?"

"How do you expect?" was the cutting response.

Kate continued, "I know this is a difficult time but we think we're almost there and we will have answers and you will have some peace."

Beth Sandford merely looked coolly down her nose. Something she could do with ease, Kate conceded.

"How are these groups set up?"

"What do you mean?"

"Are they setup by staff? By subject? Friendship groups?"

"Mainly friendship groups but with a subject element."

Looking through the lists, Kate spotted that Izzy was in a different group from Chloe and so asked for that group to be sent for. Miss Sandford went to organise that and Alice and Kate adjourned to the meeting room.

"Right, I want you to take the lead on this. I want girly chatter about the other girls here. Who's friends with whom. Who they have problems with. You know the sort of thing."

Alice paled but nodded in the affirmative.

"I'm going to be writing up notes at the back and you're waiting for me to join you at the table. That should allow casual chatter."

Plan decided, they waited.

CHAPTER 62

Soon they heard the chatter of young women and the door to the room opened. Izzy paled as she followed another girl in and saw who was in the room. Kate smiled briefly but then bent her head over her notes. Alice took over and sat the girls at one of the other tables.

"Hello, I'm Alice. DI Medlar has some questions for you but she just got to write up something whilst it's fresh in her mind."

The girls looked from one to the other. "May I ask your names, while we're waiting?"

They went around the table and gave their names. "So are you all friends or just in the same subjects?"

The girl who had entered the room first and subsequently identified as Belinda answered, "Oh all the lower sixth are friends."

"Not strictly true," Izzy offered.

"Well we've known each other forever," Claire said. And so the conversation began about degrees of friendship versus acquaintances.

Kate allowed the chatter to continue for about twenty minutes and then approached the table. "Sorry, ladies," she didn't want to use the term 'girls'. She wanted these young women to feel that she respected them.

"I just want to get a better idea of what

happened in the common room the night Kitty lost her lit text."

A couple of the girls threw a look to Izzy. "So how many of you were heads down on the task set by Ms Fleet?"

All but one girl put their hand up and she said, "I was there but working on my history assignment."

Belinda said, "Poor Kitty. She was frantic. We were busy telling her places to look."

"And she'd go dashing off and come back when she hadn't found it," added someone else.

"And I'm sure she said she'd looked in the classroom where she finally found it later," said Izzy.

"So was it Izzy who finished first or just Izzy offered to do Kitty's duty?" asked Alice.

Belinda seemed a little redder as she replied, "Izzy was one of the first to finish and she offered." Meaning you also finished but didn't offer, thought Kate.

"Does anyone know who cleared the tray away?" Kate enquired.

The girls looked at one another again. Another girl, Janice, said, "I offered to go and so did some others, so I thought someone else had done it."

Kate looked at each girl. "Anyone?" they all shook their heads. "Well thank you for your time. I apologise for the delay at the start."

Various polite comments were made as the girls departed. Once the door had closed Kate turned to Alice, "Thoughts?"

Alice stayed quiet for a while and then gave her ideas. "No-one mentioned Chloe Millar as a close friend. In fact no-one mentioned her at all but that could be because she takes different subjects to them. These girls seemed to be doing mainly art subjects and you said Chloe was a scientist."

Kate nodded. "Okay let's ask to see the next group."

CHAPTER 63

This time Alice offered to go and fetch the group and Kate could hear her chatting with the girls as they approached the meetings room. Once again Alice directed them to a table to sit. Kate called across, "Apologies, ladies. I just have to get something in order, be with you in a moment.

The conversation was pleasant but unremarkable and Chloe's name was never mentioned. Once again, after about twenty minutes, Kate joined them at the table. This time they had some information about the tray at the end of the collection. A girl called Grace said, "A number of us offered to go and collect it but I can't remember who definitely said they would and I suddenly remembered it again at about eight-thirty so I dashed up and checked whether the tray was in the kitchen and it was. Someone had collected it but I don't know who."

"Thank you Grace that does help."

"Oh and I met Jules on her way up as I was coming down. She'd had the same thought so I told her it had been done."

"What did she say?"

"Oh something like, 'Good. I couldn't remember who was supposed to be collecting it.'"

"And then what did you both do?"

"We walked back across the quad and went to

our different houses."

"Thank you all. Sorry to have torn you away from a study session." Chuckles and groans greeted this sally.

***

The final group was Chloe's group. Again Alice had been to collect them and Kate stayed at a distant desk. Whilst the chatter went on Kate surreptitiously watched Chloe. Although she was sat at the table with the girls her body language said she was not part of it. Kate noted that whereas the other girls occasionally knocked arms or tapped one another, no contact was made with Chloe. Nor did she contribute to the discussion, not even when Alice moved it on to best and favourite subjects.

No-one offered any information about who collected the tray. The only point Chloe made was on the evening of the murder she was not in the school. As a day girl she went home about six thirty. Chloe's voice when she spoke was soft, calm even. She claimed she had been in the common room that evening but hadn't really been listening to the lit group, although she'd been vaguely aware of Kitty coming in and out. "I just thought that Kitty had lost something, again." Her tone was dismissive.

Once again Kate thanked them for their help

and let them go. Was it her imagination or had Chloe glanced her way as they left?

"Okay, what do you think we have learnt about Chloe Millar?" Kate asked Alice.

Alice frowned before answering, "Not a lot. Even in that group she wasn't really part of the chatter. No-one asked for her opinion or asked her to confirm an idea or a fact. We learnt that Chloe is a lot of negatives."

Kate agreed, "And did you notice that no-one made physical or eye contact with her? They did with one another but she is clearly not part of their group."

"So pretty much what the teachers told us?"

"Well I hope Len or Colm come up with something because I really can't get a handle on this young woman."

Transcript Audio Log 1min 3secs

I don't understand it. The police found the phial. The school is in hyper drive about it and no-one is talking to Izzy. But why is she still in school? Shouldn't they be arresting her? And then on top of that all the lower sixth had to be interviewed by that police woman and she's still asking about the night of the murder. She brought a young police officer with her. Dressed in civilian clothes to try and hide who she is. But I remember her from Saturday, she was in charge of the interviewing of all the staff.

The younger one came and collected us from our study period. She chatted and the other girls responded in their inane way. DI Medlar, I know her name now, pretended to be writing up something at another table while the younger one chatted to us. I wasn't taken in. Medlar was watching all of us. They weren't going to catch me letting something slip. How moronic does she think I am?

They had the forensics team in to search Izzy's room. Did they find something I hadn't intended? No. My plan is perfect.

CHAPTER 64

Kate and Alice were the first of her team back and whilst Alice wrote up their meagre information about Chloe Millar, gleaned from her peers, Kate rung the forensic lab. She knew she was pushing her luck but Miles had said he'd put a rush on the phial. PC Bakir answered the phone, "Hi Zara, I know I'm on a long shot but has the lab got anything on a glass phial I dropped in just before lunch?"

Kate could hear tapping as Zara went through the forensic log and finally said, "I don't know what you've got over Mike, but yes the results are back. Nothing very exciting, I 'm sorry to say. The phial was wiped clean, not a smidge to dust. And as you had guessed, the contents had been ketamine."

Hearing Kate's sigh, she continued, "That's good for our whizz kid, isn't it?"

"Not really. It doesn't count her in or out. But thanks for checking and thanks for your work at the school."

"My pleasure. I learnt a lot from the spyware."

Kate put the receiver down and stared into space. This case was all about negatives; what wasn't there; what couldn't be quantified. The only positive she felt she had was that she was sure the Blaiseforth money was the ultimate motive.

She heard Hughes' and Colm's voices echoing up the stairs. Their presence was followed by that of Len. Colm, Kate noted, looked particularly pleased with himself.

Kate clapped her hands and called, "Good timing everyone. Let's have a team debrief."

Everyone made themselves comfortable at the table. Kate asked Alice to feed back their lack of detail and when she had finished Len added, "Pretty much the same from her primary school. I managed to talk to her class teacher from her reception class. Apparently Chloe was a very distant child from the off. The teacher particularly noticed that she didn't like to share and was often at the centre of disputes about whose turn it was to have something or do something."

"That's not that unusual, is it?" Kate asked, playing devil's advocate. "All kids, especially only children, have to learn to share."

Len agreed but continued, "The teacher went on to say that she thought Chloe learnt to hide it better as she got older but that she still didn't want to share."

"Do you think that was the same with her parents?" Alice asked.

"I did ask about how Chloe had been in school after the death of her brother," Len turned a page in his notebook. "She said they'd been all set up with a direct line to the school counsellor at the comp, if needed, but when Chloe returned she seemed just as before. In her words, 'you'd never have known the family had suffered such a tragedy'. She said they were very concerned about her."

Len flicked another page. "I then spoke to the Head, she was in post when Chloe was there. She said they had wondered, even before the brother's death, whether Chloe might be on 'the autistic spectrum'. She tried to talk to the parents but the mother was in a world of her own and the father rarely available. In the end she had approached the grandparents."

"The Newtons?"

"Yes. Nothing known about the father's parents. Anyway, they arranged for Chloe to see a psychiatrist. The school never heard back about the result of this and then of course Chloe moved up to Blaiseforth."

"Okay, Anything else?"

Len shut his notebook, "That's it boss."

"Good info. Thanks. Action point: we need to talk to Jack Newton about the psychiatrist."

Kate turned to Colm who grinned from ear to ear. With flair he flicked open his notebook. "I managed to have quite a long chat with Audrey Newton's one to one carer. Basically she does all the personal care, feeding her, making sure she drinks etc. The only thing she's not allowed to do is the medication. Her name is Gabby Blake."

Kate made a wind up motion with her hand, which she was sure Colm had seen but chose to ignore. He was enjoying this. "Anyway, Gabby was on duty the week before the commotion Miss Hazel mentioned, when Chloe visited. Gabby had left them alone and then, later, as she was passing Audrey's room she'd heard Chloe say, "You'll be fine. It's for the best." Thinking that Audrey might need something, Gabby had gone in to see Chloe with one of Audrey's pillows in her hands."

"Oh no!" Alice gasped.

Colm shook his head. "Apparently Chloe was very plausible and said that she thought her grandmother had become uncomfortable and she was just re-arranging her pillows. Gabby offered to do it and Chloe let her and left. Gabby says Audrey was very unsettled for the rest of the day but her speech is unclear. Apparently some words are slurred and unintelligible and even clear words are nonsense within the context."

"Did Gabby say she thought Chloe was a danger to Audrey?" Kate asked.

"She wouldn't go that far but the next visit from Chloe was the one when Audrey was terrified and screamed her head off. Gabby suggested that Chloe not visit for a while and she hasn't been back since."

"Has Audrey had that reaction to anyone else?" Len asked.

Colm shook his head. "No. She has unsettled

days when she doesn't want to talk to anyone but never the screaming abdabs."

"So when did this first incident happen?"

"Gabby wasn't exact but she knew it was the summer because she likes the view from Audrey's room and had remarked on it that day."

The room fell silent, each lost in their own thought developments. Finally Kate said, "Are we saying that an eleven year old girl killed her brother? Then tried to murder her grandmother four years later and then successfully murdered her headteacher? And on top of that could be behind a series of potentially fatal accidents and attempting to frame a school colleague?"

No-one met Kate's eyes. Alice was doodling, Len was making a show of re-reading his notes, Colm was staring out the window and Hughes was updating their murder book.

Finally, Colm dragged his eyes away from the window, "When you put it like that it seems…" He couldn't find the right word.

"A bit too much?" Alice supplied.

Colm nodded and Kate said, "And we have no evidence. If we could at least tie her to the ketamine or Gary Phipps."

Len's head jerked up and Kate turned to him. "Gary Phipps?"

"Yes, drug dealer on the Camworth."

"Yeh, I know. It's just that Phipps has a son in the reception teacher's class and she mentioned that Chloe had picked him up on a few occasions rather than Phipps or the grandmother."

"Was she sure it was Chloe Millar?"

"Yes. Apparently they will only release kids to named adults and Chloe wasn't on the list so the teacher had to phone Gary and confirm it was all legit."

Kate sat up straighter, "Colm get in touch with Terry again and find out their state of play with Phipps. I want to talk with him again, as soon as possible." Kate then turned to Alice. "Let's forget Jack Newton for the moment. Get in touch with the GP and the school and see if they know about the psychiatrist and any outcomes."

Finally turning to Len she said, "Check with the school, social services; what's the state of play with Gary and his son. Will it give us some leverage?"

They all waited for the next instruction, "We're right on the close of offices so we'll reconvene at nine thirty tomorrow. I need to go and talk to Bart. I think we may need to do a double search."

CHAPTER 65

Kate updated Bart and finished with, "So we have possible leverage with Phipps who may have supplied the ketamine but we need to search Phipps' place, Chloe's home and any lockers or the like she has at the school." Kate sat back and waited for Bart to think it through.

"Are you thinking dawn raids?"

Kate shook her head. "I want the boy and Chloe in school and I want our visits to be as low key as possible. Chloe may not have friends in school but she may have on the estate. I don't want anyone giving her the heads up."

Bart nodded. "So, why are we searching Phipps' place?"

"I'm just thinking that Chloe may not have thought that we would find the Phipps connection and so may have stored more incriminating stuff there than at her own home."

Bart nodded, agreeing with her logic, "Okay, do you want the Phipps gig?"

Kate nodded, "Yes. I want to nail him as soon as we can. He may be our only crack in Chloe's narrative."

"What about the Millars? Do you want me to lead?"

Inwardly Kate sighed, "Yes, please, sir. You'll be great at smoothing ruffled feathers, but don't go into the school, please."

Bart smiled, "No, that's your prerogative."

Bart then became very business-like. "Right, I'll pull in some extra bodies and we'll have teams of half a dozen each. You'll have Colm as back up and I'll take Jan Coles. What about Len and Alice?"

"I'll take Len and then send him back here with Phipps. You can have Alice."

Bart nodded, "Did you know it was Len who didn't secure the sitting room?"

Kate blew out her cheeks, "No. Lazy sod. But, in fairness, he has seemed to pull his finger out on this one."

"So I've heard. How are you getting Phipps here?"

"I'm going to arrest him under suspicion of being an accomplice in the murder of Elise Betteridge."

"You think that might put the fear of God into him."

Kate wrinkled her nose, "I'm not sure. He sails close to the wind and hasn't been caught yet, but his son may be his Achilles heel."

"And in turn Phipps is Chloe's!"

"Umm. Do you think I need to tell the uniforms to be thorough?"

Bart raised an eyebrow and Kate hurried on. "Chloe thinks she is smarter than us so she may well hide important evidence in plain sight. You know; the confessional diary on the shelf disguised as a science text book. That sort of thing."

Bart nodded his understanding, "I tell you what. I'll do the briefing and underline just how bright the girl is. It would be the cream indeed if we found this fabled diary!"

Kate smiled wearily. "If it exists. That's my concern; we're going to be short of evidence and I still don't know how to approach Chloe. Everyone we've spoken to has said she's a loner. Doesn't have friends. Doesn't mix. Where do I start?"

"Do you think her relationship with Phipps is a sexual one?"

Kate thought back to Phipps' leer and comment about the girl asking for the ketamine was old enough for sex. "I think so. It doesn't sit right with everything about Chloe's life. Perhaps he is special to her."

"Or perhaps he is a useful tool," Bart added. "If she did attempt to suffocate her grandmother what was her motive?"

"Money," Kate replied instantly and then more considered. "I think she thought if her grandmother was dead her grandfather would go back to paying her fees and so she could be a boarder again."

"And her brother's death? Was that about not wanting to share her parents? Wasn't sharing something she struggled with as a youngster?"

"We do need to know what the outcome of

her psychiatric sessions was."

"You're going to come up against client confidentiality," Bart warned.

"Yes. But I am going to argue that she is a danger to the public, and that the records may have pertinent information."

"Run it past the legal bods first will you. No, tell you what, I have a contact there. I'll call her as soon as we've finished."

"Thank you sir. Can I suggest that we time both searches for eleven tomorrow morning?"

"Fine. I'll update the warrant and get it authorised. All the best, Kate. We need a result."

Kate nodded her understanding. Her position, her career was on the line over this, her first murder case as senior investigating officer. Bart was already tapping in a phone number as she closed the door on his office. She was still unsure whether or not to talk to Jack Newton again. Another visit would undoubtedly flag up that Chloe was in their sights. Would he then alert his daughter? Chloe herself? No. If needs be she'd contact him tomorrow when she had Chloe in. Because tomorrow she was going to have to break Chloe Millar's armour.

CHAPTER 66

Kate knocked sharply on Gary Phipps' front door. Colm had reported back from the drugs team that although Phipps would always be a person of interest they were free to tackle him. Behind her was Colm and a group of officers wearing blue gloves. She wanted them inside as soon as possible. Bart was just a couple of roads away doing the same thing to the Millars. The door was answered by an older woman, the grandmother. Len had learnt that Phipps lived with his mother and son. That he had gained responsibility of his son, Leon, from his mother, who was a crack head. However, Social Services were involved because of Phipps' criminal record.

"Good morning, Mrs Phipps?" Kate held up her warrant card and then the search warrant. "We need to come in, please. I'd like to do it quickly and quietly so as not to alert your neighbours."

Resignedly, Mrs Phipps stood back and held the door open for them to enter. Kate made her way to the main room on the ground floor. Phipps was sat in front of the TV, dressed in much less fashionable jeans and jumper.

"Good morning Mr Phipps."

Phipps jumped up, "What the hell is this? You only raided me last week you effing idiots."

"Gary Phipps you are under arrest on suspicion of being an accomplice in the murder of Elise Betteridge. You have the right to..." Colm carried on with the spiel needed and Phipps stood there dumbfounded.

As Colm cuffed him, he sprang into life. "What do you mean an accomplice in a murder? I don't know any Betteridge. Who is she?"

"Don't worry, Gary," Kate said calmly. "We'll get you back to the station and you can call your solicitor and then we'll have a chat and I'll explain it to you." Kate turned to Len and one other officer. "Officers please take Mr Phipps back and book him in. Please impress on his solicitor that we would like to interview him as soon as possible."

Shaking his head and muttering expletives, Phipps was led out to a waiting, unmarked vehicle.

Kate turned to her colleagues and urged them to be thorough and careful. "I do not want Mrs Phipps having to spend the next few days putting everything back."

She followed Mrs Phipps into the kitchen. The woman sat down wearily at a small table stuck in the corner. "You won't find nothing," she began and then added, "but if you do it'll be that little bitch's."

"Who would that be, Mrs Phipps?"

"That Chloe Millar. Miss hoity toity. She leads him round by his you know what. And I don't mean his nose!"

Despite herself Kate smiled as the woman continued. "I've told him, she's only into him because he can provide things for her but she'll get rid of him as soon as he's no more use. I wouldn't trust her further than I could spit her!"

"How long have they been an item, Gary and Chloe?"

"Oh, I dunno. She started dropping in here last summer and then she began stopping over. He's blinded by her supposed intelligence and whatever else they get up to," she rocked her eyes suggestively upward towards the bedrooms.

"So what do you think she wants from Gary?"

Now Mrs Phipps became cagey. Kate saw that she was well aware of her son's 'business interests'. "Not sure, but whatever it was… Is… He didn't know what she was planning."

"And what was that, Mrs Phipps."

"Haven't got the foggiest. But why else would a girl like her hook up with my Gary. I may be his mother but I'm not blind to his faults."

Whatever else Kate may have got out of Mrs Phipps was interrupted by Colm's voice calling her from the stairs. He was stood halfway up and nodded his head upwards. "You'll want to see this, boss."

The back bedroom was clearly Phipps' room and it showed signs of female occupancy. In one corner an officer was hunkered down looking at the skirting board. Kate could see that there was a fairy door on it. She'd bought her six year old niece one last Christmas but what was one doing in an adult male's bedroom? The officer waited until Kate was peering over her shoulder and then removed the door. Behind was a small hole in the brickwork. The officer put her fingers in and removed two glass phials. Careful not to smudge possible fingerprints she held each by the very tips of her fingers and dropped each into its own evidence bag. Once each was sealed and written on, she handed them to Kate.

Colm and Kate grinned at each other. Holding each bag up it was clear that these were the mates to the one they found in Izzy's room. Kate whispered, "Oh, I hope she was careless enough to leave fingerprints."

"I don't think she expected us to make the connection between her and Phipps."

"Okay keep searching. I know Bart scoffed but I do wonder if there is a diary or something similar somewhere. She would have been too careful to tell anyone, even Phipps, exactly what she was doing. Or why. But I think she would have needed to have some outlet. What's better than Dear Diary?"

CHAPTER 67

The searchers were thorough and tidy but no further finds were of interest. Kate thanked Mrs Phipps for her patience and headed back to the station. On the way back her phone rang. It was Bart. "Hello, sir. How did it go?"

Kate could hear the smile in his voice, "I think we may have found you some evidence."

Trying to put a lid on her excitement Kate tried to suppress the whoop that was threatening to escape her chest. "We found some as well, sir. Hidden in Phipps' bedroom."

"Okay Kate. We're on our way back to the station. We'll compare trophies then.

"Thanks, sir. We're on our way, too."

Bart was waiting in their incident room when Colm and Kate returned. He had a small evidence bag in front of him. Kate added their two to his.

"Okay Kate, what have you got?" He held up Kate's bags and smiled. "She may claim that they're nothing to do with her if they were found in Phipps' room."

Kate agreed, "Fingerprints would be the icing. What about your evidence, sir." She couldn't clearly see inside his bag but it seemed like a pen!" He held it up for Kate to have a closer look. It was a pen. Kate was baffled and Bart grinned.

"I think we'll have to promote PC Giles. She found it."

"Alice? But how is it evidence?" At that point Alice herself appeared.

"Ah, the star of the moment," Bart was really quite elated by his find. "Show her how it works."

Alice took the bag and manipulated the pen and suddenly Kate's heart missed a beat as the voice of, she assumed, their murder victim could be heard. "No, Chloe. I have gone against my better judgement agreeing to ask your teachers to support your application. Now you will go against the other entrants on your own merit. I have withdrawn from the panel."

Alice clicked it off. "We haven't heard it all but we have sampled sections of it and it seems to be a mix of secret recordings of meetings she's had with people, including, Gary Phipps and also some sort of audio diary."

Kate sat down and the air left her body, "Our fabled confessional diary!"

"But how did you know what it was?" Colm asked.

Alice blushed, "I... er... I read this crime novel and there was a journalist that had one and I thought it was nifty so looked online. They're not as expensive as you'd think."

"Yeh, but how did you know this was one of them?" Kate asked.

"Two things really. One was that I think

Chloe was being too clever. The pen was balanced on her desk with the clip face up. We all know that if you casually put down a pen it will roll onto the clip side." Alice looked around for confirmation.

"Not sure I've ever thought about it," said Colm with furrowed brow.

"Well, it just looked wrong and then when I took a closer look I saw the maker's name and it was one I recognised from my surfing about dictapens."

"Amazing!" said Kate with feeling. "Right, Alice and Colm get these things to forensics. I want a copy of the recording, now. Then someone can work on the transcription. I want everything dusted for fingerprints."

"Yes boss," they chorused.

As they left the room Bart said, "Can I have a word, Kate?"

She turned back to him, "Yes, sir?"

"I don't want to tell you how to run this investigation but I think you need to get Chloe into custody. No matter how low key we were today someone will have noticed and may already have warned her. And her mother will let her know what we've got."

Kate's face fell. "I really wanted to have a go with Phipps before I brought Chloe in." She chased thoughts around and then began to nod, "But no, you're right. We need to get Chloe in."

"Why don't you interview Phipps and I'll

take Alice to collect Chloe from school? By the time we have either a suitable adult or a solicitor you'll know what you can get out of Phipps."

Kate was going to protest but Bart held a hand up. "I know technically she doesn't need a suitable adult, but let's be above board in all this. It might make her think that we think she's still a child."

Kate wasn't sure but she thought Bart may have a point about keeping Chloe off her guard. "Yes, sir. Thank you."

CHAPTER 68

Once again Colm and Kate entered the interview room with Gary Phipps in, carrying two cups a piece. "Hello, Gary. Mr Forbes. Tea again?" Kate pushed a cup towards Phipps.

Kate noted that he didn't look as calm and patient as he had when the drugs team had pulled him in. Kate sat and shuffled through her papers. She and Colm had decided that Gary might respond to the feminine touch but he was ready to step in if that failed.

"Okay, Gary, is it okay to call you Gary or would you prefer Mr Phipps?"

A shrugged shoulder and, "I don't care what you call me as long as we get this sorted out. What's this about murder?"

Kate smiled, she hoped, sympathetically. "We will get to that point Gary but I need to fill in some background details first. Can you confirm who lives with you?"

Gary sighed deeply and fidgeted in his chair. The suave man of the town was gone. "I live with my mother and my son."

Kate nodded as she appeared to be checking the information with what she had in her papers. "Do you have a girlfriend, Gary? Someone who stops over?"

"What if I have?"

"So you do have a girlfriend? And does she stop over?"

"Sometimes." It was clear on his face that he was trying to work out where this questioning was going. "What has that got to with anything?"

"We're just trying to establish who would have access to your bedroom."

"My bedroom?"

A string of expletives followed and Colm stepped in, "Keep it clean, Phipps."

Mr Forbes also had leant forward and whispered something in his client's ear. Phipps shrugged again and made an effort to relax in his chair.

Kate carried on with her kindly approach, "I understand your question, Gary, but you see the reason I needed to establish who had access to your room is that we found something in it which shouldn't have been there."

Phipps' face went blank. Kate thought he knew what they had found. He may not have known that Chloe had hidden them in his room but he knew what she had to hide.

"Would you like to make a guess at what we found?"

Phipps bowed his shoulder but didn't reply and Kate continued, "Now my concern, Gary, is that this will put in jeopardy your custody of Leon."

Phipps' head shot up. "This has nothing to do

with me or Leon."

"But you can see my problem, can't you, Gary? We find a substance hidden, very carefully hidden, in your room and we know that the same substance was used in a murder. What can I do but think you had something to do with it?"

Phipps' head began to shake from side to side. Kate could barely hear his muttering but it sounded like, "The silly bitch! The lying stupid bitch!"

"Sorry Gary, I didn't catch that."

Phipps took in a deep breath and looked Kate directly in the eye. "I'd like a consult with my solicitor, please."

Kate nodded and gave the time before turning off the recording device. She and Colm left the room. No sooner was the door shut than Colm asked, "What do you think? Is he going to cough up?"

"I'm not sure, but he didn't sound too enamoured of Chloe as I told him what we'd found."

Kate had only just got back from checking on the progress with forensics when Mr Forbes asked them to re-join him and his client. Once they were all sat and the recording device rolling, Mr Forbes cleared his throat. "My client would like to make a statement that will reveal the facts about the findings at his home and his total innocence in relation to anything that happened."

Kate nodded and Phipps leant forward. "I don't want to lose Leon. I really didn't know what she was up to. I promise."

"You're going to have to be much clearer than that, Phipps," Colm said.

Phipps put his clasped hands on the desk between them. With head bowed he began, "Chloe Millar moved to the estate a couple of years ago. I saw her around but nothing much. Then, about nine months ago she began to search me out, pretending she just happened to be wherever I was."

He cleared his throat and Kate saw a flush beginning below his jaw line. "She was very… seductive and we became involved."

"I'm assuming 'involved' means you started a sexual relationship?" Kate clarified.

Phipps nodded but Kate said, "For the benefit of the tape, Gary would you answer that question, please."

"Yes. I don't know where she learnt what she did but I'd never met anyone like her." By now his cheeks were aflame. He cleared his throat again, "Anyway about Christmas time she was in a right strop and said that some teacher at school was giving her a hard time and how she'd like to pay her back." Phipps shrugged again. "I didn't really think anything about it. Then she walked in on me and… a business associate who wanted me to take on some merchandise. I told him I wasn't interested but Chloe said she'd take something off him."

Kate wanted specifics and so interrupted, "We're not interested in who but I want to know what, Gary."

"She bought three glass bottles of ketamine." He held his hands up. "It was nothing to do with me."

"Didn't you ask her what she was going to do with them?" Colm could not keep the credulity out of his voice.

"Of course I did," snapped back Phipps. "She said she'd research what the drug would do, because she'd heard it was used on the streets and then she'd slip some to the teacher. Really show her up. Perhaps even get her the sack."

"And that didn't worry you?" Kate asked.

Another shrug. "I knew street ketamine. It's no more lethal than any other drug and I knew Chloe would do all the research. She's a science buff and really intelligent. She'd make sure she knew what she was doing."

"Just so I have got this right," Kate asked, "Chloe Millar bought three phials of ketamine and said she was planning to slip some to Miss Betteridge to show her up?"

Yet another shrug. "If phials is the same thing as bottles, then yes. But I didn't know the teacher's name."

"Didn't alarm bells ring when you heard about a death at the school?" Colm asked.

Phipps shook his head. "Everyone was saying

it was a heart attack. I didn't think it was Chloe's teacher. She never said it was the Head she had a beef with."

Kate rose. "Thank you, Gary. You'll remain in custody while we check out your information."

"But..." Whatever Phipps was going to say was prevented by a warning hand on his arm from his solicitor.

Kate finished the recording and left with Colm in her wake.

CHAPTER 69

"Well, we've got confirmation of Chloe buying the stuff," said Colm as they headed back to the incident room.

"Umm. But will he testify in court, if we had to?"

Passing Bart's office door, she popped her head in and saw him sat at his desk… "Chloe in?"

"Yes. I've put her in the children's suite. Play it low key."

Kate nodded her agreement, "What about an appropriate adult?"

"Yes. Guess who she's gone for?"

"Her dad?" Kate hazarded a guess.

"Nope, her granddad!"

"Jack Newton!"

"I thought it was an interesting choice. I've rung him and he's on his way in. What about Phipps?"

"He's confirmed that Chloe bought and hid the ketamine. According to him she was going to research its effects and slip it to a teacher she hated. Just to show her up."

Bart shook his head in wonderment. "Well, let's hope Chloe is as forthcoming."

Kate left the office and followed Colm back to the incident room. Alice was already at work at her desk and turned as Kate entered. "Zara has downloaded the recordings and separated them into topics. They're on your network."

"Thanks Alice," Kate opened up her browser and clicked on the network. As promised there was a single folder, which when clicked on, revealed a number of smaller files: Diary. Planning. Interviews. Kate clicked on Diary and slipped on a set of headphones, plugging them in.

She heard, "I learnt from an early age that if I wanted something I needed to do it for myself. My brother is a case in point. Why would anyone want to share their parents with a squalling, shitting little monster?" A shiver ran through Kate and she switched it off. The calm, calculating tone was unnerving. Perhaps she would wait for the transcript and weed out what she didn't need at this stage.

She called across to Alice, "How long before the transcript is done?"

"Not long. It's all computerised. I finally managed to talk to the psychiatrist who saw Chloe when she was eleven."

"Oh good. No problems about confidentiality?"

"Not really. I asked if he thought Chloe was autistic and he said no. Most definitely not, but wouldn't go into detail. He also said that Chloe only attended two sessions and then Mrs Millar cancelled any further sessions claiming that they unsettled Chloe rather than helped."

"So nothing of any great importance, then?"

"I did ask him if he thought Chloe may be suffering from a personality disorder. He didn't answer directly but said that she was too young to make definitive diagnosis at eleven but he would be interested to meet with her now as she is growing into adulthood. The way he phrased it just made me think he thought there was something there."

"Okay. It's something." Any further conversation was prevented by simultaneous pings on each of their computers. The transcript had arrived. It ran to ninety-three pages. Seeing the number, Kate called out to Colm and Alice. "We need to divide this between us. Alice you take Diary, Colm take Interviews and I'll tackle Planning."

Twenty minutes later Kate's desk phone rang and she answered it. "Thank you. Put him in with Chloe and get them some refreshments. We'll be down in ten."

Kate turned to the room. "Okay. Jack Newton has arrived. Anybody got anything concrete we can use? Alice?"

"She killed her brother with a silk handkerchief! Held it across his face until he stopped moving. She didn't like the psychiatrist because he wanted to know how she felt about her brother. Not his death, which she was ready for, but when he was alive. I'm at the point where she is manipulating all the adults to get her into

Blaiseforth Manor."

"She definitely says she killed her brother?"

"Oh yes. She had it all planned out. The only thing she hadn't predicted was her mother falling apart and the impact that had."

Kate turned to Colm. "Who does she record?"

"There are two interviews with our victim. In both she is vile and, as we thought, used the relationship with her grandfather as leverage. But in the second interview our victim is quite clear that she will not be blackmailed and that Chloe would win the Blaiseforth Prize under her own merit not from manipulating the panel."

"Thus signing her own death warrant!"

"There's a couple of recordings with some of the other girls at the school but I think she was either checking out how well the device worked or they were recorded in error."

"Right. Before we go down I want to check with forensics on fingerprints." Kate dialled and waited. "Hi, Mike. Any news on our new evidence? Okay. Thanks. Let Alice know and she can bring it to me if it's relevant." Kate replaced the receiver. "Come on then, Colm. Time to visit our suspect."

CHAPTER 70

Before they entered the interview room Kate took a look at their suspect through the two way mirror. She noted that Jack Newton was sat on a sofa at an angle to where Chloe sat. He was not in physical contact with her and neither was she allowing eye contact. They heard Jack ask Chloe, "What's it all about, love?"

"I don't know. They think I had something to do with Miss Betteridge's death."

Kate whispered to Colm, "Go and check with Bart what he said to Chloe when he bought her in. He was going to play it really low key and no accusations." As Colm slipped back out the door she added, "And check whether she's been fingerprinted."

Kate continued to watch. Chloe looked calm and unconcerned. No anxiety, no tears. It was Jack who showed his concern. Rubbing his face with his hands and shaking his head in confusion. A few minutes later Colm reappeared. "Bart says he was very low key. Asked her if she could come and clarify some details about the Monday evening and Kitty's lost book. And yes to fingerprinting."

"Okay then. I think that until we have confirmation of fingerprints we play this really low key. I am going to start with what a tough childhood she has and work our way through."

"That's going to be really tough on her granddad. Should we suggest a different appropriate adult?"

"I don't think we can. We'll keep an eye on Jack and see how he's coping. We may have to suggest a change." Kate gave an ironic smile, "Someone's going to leave that room very unhappy. I don't want it to be us."

Colm nodded and they headed for the interview room.

Kate smiled broadly as she entered. "Hello, Chloe, we've only met briefly but I'm DI Kate Medlar and this is my colleague DC Hunter." Kate then turned to Jack Newton and held out her hand, "Hello again, Mr Newton." Jack shook the proffered hand but looked apprehensive.

Colm followed suit. They had planned to differentiate between Jack as the appropriate adult and Chloe as a youngster. They'd hoped it would make her relax her guard if she thought that they thought she was only a child. If it antagonised her they'd work with it.

Having sat down Kate turned to Jack and explained his role as an appropriate adult and concluded with, "The main thing is please do not answer for Chloe or assume you know her answers. If you think the question is inappropriate then please tell us." Jack nodded and looked anxiously at Chloe who seemed quite relaxed.

Kate turned to Chloe, "Okay Chloe, anything you don't understand then please let us know. We're not here to confuse you or trip you up. We just want your view of things. Is that all right?"

Chloe looked at a point over Kate's left shoulder and replied, "Yes, I understand."

"I understand from your granddad and your teachers that you've had a difficult childhood."

Chloe merely looked. Kate saw little light in her eyes.

"So, I hope it won't upset you too much if we revisit some of those occasions."

Jack Newton shifted in his chair. He wasn't sure where Kate was going or what she wanted to ask. A warning look from Colm stopped any question emerging.

"How old were you when Daniel died?"

"Inspector, I fail to see..." Jack erupted.

"Thank you Mr Newton but I just want to understand Chloe's life a little better." Kate turned back to Chloe who now looked directly at Kate, unsure what was happening. This was clearly not what she had been expecting. "What age were you, Chloe?"

"Eleven."

"It must have been tough," Chloe had started to nod when Kate continued, "to put up with another child when you were used to having your mum and dad to yourself." Chloe froze. Kate could see a question start to form but Chloe bit down on her lip and merely shrugged.

"How did your parents prepare you for the arrival of a baby? Praise you as how good you'd be as a big sister?"

"Oh yes. How lucky I was to be going to have a baby brother!" Chloe couldn't keep the scorn out of her voice and Jack twitched as he heard it.

"They do tend to cry and shit a lot, don't they?" Kate had paraphrased Chloe's own description, she didn't want to give away that they'd found her audio diary, yet. Even so Chloe's look sharpened at Kate's words.

"So how did you feel when Daniel arrived?" Colm asked.

Chloe switched her gaze to him but didn't answer.

"He didn't really fit into your plans did he?" Kate persisted.

"In a strange way his death was the best thing to happen to me," Chloe said. Jack audibly gasped and Chloe turned to him and Kate was sure she saw Chloe put on the little granddaughter personality, "Only because it meant I got to go to Blaiseforth Manor, Granddad. You always say 'look for the silver lining'."

Jack Newton nodded but Kate thought he looked uncomfortable with her response.

Suddenly Chloe said, "I need the toilet."

"No problem." Stating the time and the break

Kate stopped the interview and called for the uniform outside to take Chloe to the facilities.

CHAPTER 71

Once Chloe was back in the room, Kate restarted the recording and continued, "So a lot of people made a lot of sacrifices for you to go to Blaiseforth, didn't they?"

Chloe looked genuinely confused so Kate listed them, "The death of Daniel." She ticked off a finger, "Your mother's breakdown." Another finger. "Your grandparents selling up and giving money for your fees. Your parents selling up and moving to Camworth. A lot of sacrifices, don't you think?"

Chloe shrugged, "Yes. I suppose so."

"Of course your grandparents couldn't help once your grandma was too ill to stay at home, could they? That must have been tough for you. Dragged out of school because they couldn't pay the fees."

Colour had flared in Chloe's cheeks and, for the first time, Kate saw life in her eyes. "It was humiliating."

"But you did get to go back," Colm suggested reasonably.

Chloe's eyes really did flash as she turned on him. "Oh yes. Back as a day girl. No longer part of the school in the same way. And some of them were real bitches."

Jack mumbled, "Oh, Chloe, love."

Chloe's gaze at her granddad was one of pure scorn.

"I understand Kitty and Izzy warned them off, though. That must have made life better?" Kate said.

Shrugged, "I suppose so."

"It sounds like you didn't appreciate their interference," Kate queried.

"I was fine. They're just a pair of do-gooders."

"But worthy adversaries in the Blaiseforth Prize?" Colm asked.

"Well I need the money more than they do!" was the sharp reply.

Kate decided to change tack, "It must have been hard on you when your grandmother screamed if you went near her."

Kate decided a patronising look settled on Chloe's face. "It is a terrible disease. Poor Grandma. She doesn't know anyone any more," turning to Jack, "does she, Granddad?"

"But it's only you she seems frightened of." Colm persisted, "Why is that do you think?"

Chloe shrugged again and Kate decided to reveal her hand, "Might it have something to do with the fact that you tried to smother her with her own pillow?"

Out of the corner of her eye, Kate saw a look of horror creep over Jack's face. Horror at the suggestion or horror that it might be true? He looked hard at his granddaughter, especially as she did not dismiss Kate's accusation.

Finally Chloe responded, "You seem to have a very vivid imagination, DI Medlar."

"Oh, I've no imagination!" Kate smiled, "I only ever base my ideas on facts."

The supercilious smile that had been growing on Chloe's face began to die. Chloe was calculating. Kate was sure of that and decided to change tack again.

"Tell us when you knew of your granddad's relationship with Miss Betteridge?"

Jack leant forward abruptly, "She never knew."

The roll of Chloe's eyes, typical of a teenager, stopped him. "Of course I did, Granddad. I heard you tell Mum at Christmas."

Deflated he sat back and mumbled, "I didn't realise."

Colm interrupted, "Mr Newton could I remind you about what DI Medlar said about the role of the appropriate adult."

"How did you feel about their friendship?"

Chloe shrugged nonchalantly. "Didn't really bother me."

"What did Miss Betteridge say when you told her you knew?"

Now Kate had her attention. Kate could see the calculations going on behind the eyes. How much did they know? Especially since Kate's comment about only basing ideas on facts. Had someone seen her going into the Head's office?

What should she admit to?

She gambled, "I never told her I knew. I haven't spoken to Miss Betteridge since I came back to the school."

Got you! Kate thought. If Chloe had left it at 'I never told her', they'd have been stuck but the added sentence told the lie. Kate made a show of surprise and made a performance of checking through her notes. "That's strange. I have two independent sources who say that you spoke to Miss Betteridge about entering the Blaiseforth Prize at the start of term."

"Really! I thought you were encouraged to enter by your teachers," interrupted Jack.

"Well, once I talked to her, they did."

Infuriating as Jack's comments were this did actually move them forward. "So you did speak to Miss Betteridge at the start of term?" Kate persisted.

"Yes. I forgot." Chloe sulked.

"How could you forget you spoke with her when the prize means so much to the girls at your school?" Kate allowed her tone to carry some sense of disbelief.

"I just forgot." A stubbornness was evident in her tone and her body language.

Kate moved on. "We'll come back to that later. Now I understand that your boyfriend is Gary Phipps?"

That caught Chloe's attention. Had she not reckoned that they would find the connection?

Now she sat straighter and her look became wary. "Yes. So what?"

"How long have you been seeing him?"

"Oh about three or four months."

"Good looking chap. Did you chase him or he you?"

Again that teenage eye roll. "We just met up a few times and we liked each other. No big deal."

"Do you sleep over very often at Gary's place?"

"Not normally school nights. Mainly at the weekend."

"So, do you keep stuff at his place? Save having to pack too many things each time?"

Chloe looked wary again. Kate guessed she was wondering if they know about her hidey-hole?

"I've left a few bits and pieces, a toothbrush, a hairbrush, some bits of make-up. Not a lot really."

At that moment there was a tap at the door and then it opened to show Alice with a sheaf of papers.

Kate turned back to Chloe and Jack. "My apologies but I will need to deal with this. Whilst I'm gone can I get an officer to bring you any drinks?"

Both said no and Colm and Kate left the room.

CHAPTER 72

Outside, Alice was grinning. "Fingerprints galore!"

Kate led the way through to the viewing room and reached a hand out for Alice's paper. She quickly read the papers and then looked up grinning. "She banked on us not making the connection with Phipps. Her prints are on the fairy door, the two phials and the dictapen."

"And the contents of the phials?" Colm asked.

Kate flicked through and then read, "Contents of each phial is ketamine, consistent with the chemical make-up reported on the missing vet phials and the stomach contents of our victim."

"So are you going to tell her what we've got and see what she says?" asked Alice.

"No. We keep this light. I want to see where she wants us to go. But at least we now know we were right. Back in Colm."

"Sorry about that interruption," Kate said as she and Colm returned and sat. "Where were we? I know. The ketamine you hid in Gary's bedroom."

Chloe's face was immediately alert. "I…"

Kate talked over her. "To save you embarrassment let me tell you what I have just been told by our forensic team." Kate made a show of finding the information and reading it carefully. She then looked up. "Your fingerprints are all over the fairy door, a clever idea that, and on the two phials of ketamine. So why did you buy it, Chloe?"

There was a tense silence and Chloe slumped on the sofa and looked down, "Someone asked me to."

"Okay, who?"

"I can't tell you."

Jack Newton stepped in, "Come on Chloe love. This is serious. You can't take the blame for someone else's actions."

Kate's heart went out to him. He was going to be so shocked by the time they finished. Kate waited and finally Chloe said, "Izzy Grey. She asked me to get it."

"Did she say what she wanted it for?"

Chloe shrugged, "She wanted to get her own back on one of the teachers. She didn't say who."

"So when we, the police started asking about a death in the school it didn't occur to you that this might be something to do with Izzy? Especially as she took Miss Betteridge's supper tray in?"

Chloe had been rubbing her eyes and now looked up, they were red and watery and Chloe attempted a choked voice, "I didn't want to believe she had anything to do with it."

Kate was not convinced with the act but decided to move on. "Can you explain why you were coming down from Miss Betteridge's landing on the evening of Miss Betteridge's death?"

Again Kate was sure she could see Chloe calculating. Who had seen her? When? Early in the evening when she'd set the tray up or later after she'd suffocated their victim? Kate gave her some help, "You were seen."

"I..."

"Come on love. Explain yourself." Jack was becoming uneasy.

"I... er went to see Miss Betteridge but there was no reply when I knocked at her door."

"What sort of time was that?" Colm asked.

A dagger's glance before Chloe replied, "It was early in the evening. I'm not sure of the exact time but I think it was before seven."

Lucky guess, Kate thought. "Did you collect the supper tray later that evening?"

In an exasperated tone Chloe replied, "I told you before, DI Medlar, I went home about seven-thirty."

Kate checked her notes, "I thought you said six-thirty?"

Chloe stared over Kate's shoulder for a few minutes, "I normally leave school at about six-thirty but I think it was closer to seven-thirty on Monday."

Kate let that pass. "Did you go home or to Gary's?"

Again that calculating look. What did they

know? Before Chloe could answer there was yet another knock at the door and Alice looked in. Once again Kate stopped the interview and joined Alice in the hall. "Sorry, boss, but I thought you'd want this bit of information." Alice passed a single sheet.

Kate read and passed it on to Colm. "Okay. I think we stop pussy footing around. Let's get this over and done with. Thanks Alice."

Their re-entry into the interview room interrupted an urgent discussion between Chloe and Jack. Although the urgency seemed to be more on Jack's side than Chloe's.

Kate apologised again and then launched another question, "When were you last in Miss Betteridge's sitting room, Chloe?"

"I've never been in there."

"Not even to take her supper tray?"

"I'm a day girl. We aren't put on the rota." There was an underlying bitterness in her answer.

"So, can you explain why we have your prints on Miss Betteridge's chair in her sitting room? A print that is less than a fortnight old." Kate threw in the last in the hope she was right.

Jack looked dumbfounded as he looked from Chloe to Kate and back again. "Chloe?"

Chloe seemed not to have heard. "I've always known that if I wanted anything I had to do it for myself." She seemed to be appealing to Kate, "You do understand how I had to do it all myself?"

Kate nodded. "Is that why Daniel had to die?"

"All that fuss!" A note of disgust. "Why would they think I'd want a baby brother?" A genuine query. "No-one had any time for me any more. It was like I didn't exist. Don't wake Daniel. No you can't sit on my lap with Daniel."

For a moment Kate could hear the cries of a small child and then a cooler voice took over. "He didn't suffer. I held the silk tight and he stopped crying and fighting me."

Jack Newton was white. He staggered from his chair barely managing to say, "I'm sorry I need the toilet."

CHAPTER 73

Kate sent the uniform in to sit with Chloe whilst she and Colm waited for Jack in the corridor. When he finally re-emerged he looked decidedly grey and Kate was concerned for his health but before she could make any suggestion Jack said, I can't sit in there with Chloe. I don't recognise her!" The last was almost a cry.

Kate lay a hand on his arm. "It's alright, Jack. We can get someone else to be the appropriate adult and I'll get someone to take you home."

Jack shook his head. "No. I need to talk to her father." He looked absently at the door to the interview room and then turned to Kate, "This is going to be bad, isn't it?"

"I think so, Jack. We have quite a lot of evidence now that points to Chloe's involvement in a number of activities, none of them legal and one of them concerns Elise's death."

Tears sprung to his eyes. Kate didn't know if it was for the death of Elise or the death of the granddaughter he thought he had.

Colm said, "If you come this way, Mr Newton, I can find you somewhere to make your call from."

As Colm led him away Jack looked back over his shoulder and cried, "I know I'm letting her down."

Kate called after Colm, "Explain the role of the Youth Offending Team to Mr Millar, Colm. They'll be the ones who need to attend if the parents can't."

Colm raised his hand in acknowledgement as he led Jack Newton away.

Kate went back into the interview room and arranged for Chloe to be taken to a cell. "Just until we have an appropriate adult," Kate explained. "Your Granddad has been taken ill."

Chloe seemed indifferent as she was led from the room.

***

Back in the incident room Kate relayed to the team the basics from the interview. "So she admitted it? Just like that?" Len seemed surprised.

Colm had just entered and heard this and answered, "No, not just like that. The boss got her to that point. Well done boss!"

Kate smiled but said, "It was all about what we, the team, had put together."

"Nah. It was that comment about not having any imagination, only facts that really got to her. She suddenly realised that this was not a game where she had the winning hand."

"Maybe." Kate conceded.

"So you've now got to wait for another appropriate adult? The father?" Alice asked.

Colm answered. "Mr Millar, having heard what has come out so far said he didn't think he could be present, although he is coming to the station so I explained that we would get in touch with the Youth Offending Team."

Colm directly addressed Kate, "I told him the seriousness of the case and they're sending one of their senior officers."

Kate nodded, "What about Jack?"

"I got him a decent cup of tea and he's waiting in reception for Mr Millar. I think he's torn between running away and staying and being supportive."

"Poor man," said Alice, shaking her head.

***

Gill Smith, from the Youth Offending Team, was a large lady both in height and build. She smiled broadly as she introduced herself to Kate. She had already spoken with Mr Millar and Jack Newton and had an idea of the seriousness of the crimes Kate's team were dealing with.

"You'll want to have a chat with Chloe before we start again?"

"Yes please. Just to explain who I am and why I'm here." Her accent was straight from the Camworth Estate. Kate wondered how Chloe would respond to this woman.

Kate led Gill to the interview room and signalled for the desk Sergeant to alert custody to bring Chloe up."

Leaving Gill alone, Kate returned to the incident room. "Okay Colm, ten minutes and we'll go down.

"What's the YOT officer like?"

"Seems to be down to earth. Not fazed by the severity of what we're dealing with. Should be fine."

CHAPTER 74

Kate explained again to Chloe that Gill was there as an appropriate adult but it was up to Chloe to answer as honestly as she could. Kate noted that Chloe's face was closed down and her body language was tight. She didn't even look at Gill when Kate mentioned why she was there.

"Okay Chloe, you were explaining why you were angry with Miss Betteridge."

"Was I?"

Damn, Kate thought. Was she going to have to break Chloe down now she'd had time to think?

"Yes. You were saying how you always needed to act for yourself and that Miss Betteridge was not being helpful with the Blaiseforth Prize."

Finally, Chloe sat up straight and looked directly at Kate, "She wouldn't let me win the Blaiseforth Prize. It isn't as though it was her own money, but she wouldn't. Said I wasn't good enough. That I wasn't in the same league as Kitty and Izzy."

"Did she actually say that? Didn't she say you would have to compete on your own merit?" Kate wanted clarification.

Chloe thought a little. Once again Kate had deliberately let slip a word from the recordings

Chloe had made. "She didn't see that it wasn't a level playing field so I decided to level it up," Chloe actually smiled as she said this and clearly had a particular thought in mind.

Kate hoped she was following and said, "You mean Kitty's 'accidents'."

Chloe's eyebrows went up. "Ah! I thought they had slipped below your radar."

Kate adopted a dismissive tone, "You rather overplayed your hand there. Too many too soon. Careless!"

Chloe bridled, "The stupid bitch wouldn't take a fall."

"But many of those falls would only have worked for you if they'd been fatal. Was that your intention?"

"Well, if it happened, it happened. I just wanted her out of action for enough time to be out of the running for the prize."

Kate felt a coldness run down her spine. Was Chloe really that blasé about the possible death of another girl?

Another change of tack. "Why did you buy the ketamine for Izzy?"

A shrug, "She asked."

"So are you the go to girl in the school for contraband?"

"Not really."

"So why did Izzy ask you? You said she wasn't a friend, so why risk not only your place in the school but also problems with the police if you were caught."

"Just thought I'd try. See if I could do it."

"Okay. Did Izzy know Gary Phipps was your boyfriend? Is that why she asked you? Knew he could get the stuff? No real challenge for you, really, was there?" Again, Kate tried for the dismissive tone.

Chloe responded to the deliberate pricking of her ego. "I bought the stuff, not Gary. He was all for not touching it. Too hot." Sarcasm spilled over the last sentence.

"So you gave a phial to Izzy and then she constructed this brilliant crime. No-one would have known Miss Betteridge's death was anything other than a heart attack if it wasn't for a very observant pathologist. I have to say I have a grudging admiration for Izzy in all this."

"Not so clever to get caught with the empty bottle, though, was she?"

"Really! Our forensic team found nothing." The truth since Kate had already removed the phial.

"What? They couldn't have missed…" Chloe stopped and scowled at Kate.

"Why couldn't they have missed it Chloe?"

Chloe slumped back in her chair. She seemed sunk in thought and Kate was about to ask another question when she said. "It was my plan."

"So, planting evidence was about getting Izzy out of the way for the Blaiseforth Prize?"

The tiniest of nods. "You do know that if the panel feels that no-one meets the standard necessary for the prize then they can refuse to award it?"

Chloe's head shot up and her mouth dropped open. It obviously had not occurred to her. "The bitch didn't tell me that."

"Who would that be? Miss Betteridge?"

"Yes. All that hard work and I still might not get it."

Kate noted the present tense. Chloe was still convinced that she would be competing for the prize. What world was she living in?

"Was it Miss Betteridge's resigning from the panel that led you to using the ketamine on her?"

"Well, I showed her how good I am." An element of pride, even now.

"Chloe, can you explain why you used the film wrap as well as the ketamine, to kill Miss Betteridge?"

For once a note of, was it shame? "I couldn't work out how much to give to kill her. She was still alive when I went in so I used the film wrap as a back-up."

"Did Miss Betteridge know what you were doing?" Colm asked.

"No. Shame really. I would have liked her to know what was happening and why. See if she could see the merit in me then." The sarcasm again but no regret.

Gently Kate interceded, "Chloe, do you

understand that you are admitting to the murder of Miss Betteridge?"

Chloe looked at her, no calculations now just a small smile, "Yes."

"Chloe, do you understand that you will be charged with the murder of Miss Betteridge and your brother, Daniel. With the attempted murder of Katherine Hardcastle and for perverting the course of justice."

Chloe shrugged and Kate nodded to Colm to begin the ritual phrases for arrest before taking her back to custody. Kate then looked at Gill Smith who looked pale and a little sweaty. As their eyes met, she said, "I've been in with a murderer before but nothing like this."

"What do you think, unchecked ego or is she a sociopath?" asked Kate.

Gill shook her head. "She's too calculating for a sociopath. May be a psychopath. Certainly some form of personality disorder. Do you think she'll stand trial?"

Kate shook her head. Not my decision. I'll present our case to CPS and they'll decide where it goes from there."

"I'll help with her transfer to Young Offenders."

"Thanks."

Gill Smith left and Kate continued to sit. Her first murder as senior investigating officer but she felt none of the joy she had witnessed in her colleagues when they'd got a confession. She did wonder whether Chloe's case would come to trial and how her poor family would cope. There were so many victims in this case and she hadn't given closure to all of them.

EPILOGUE

Transcript Audio Log 38secs

I want to be a boarder again. I like being part of the whole school. I don't care about the other girls, it's the school that counts. But Granddad won't pay until Grandma dies. I mean in every way but breathing she is already dead, so I sent her an anonymous box of chocolates. Her favourites, soft centres and her favourite body lotion. Just with a little addition.

Did you know every part of the yew tree is poisonous, except the flesh of the berries? Taxine alkaloids. It's amazing how easy it is to boil up the seeds. I wasn't sure how toxic my potion was but next door's cat died, so it must be quite good and Gran will get a double dose if she eats the chocolates and they use the body lotion on her. This time it will be a heart attack!

WRITING AS LIN POOK

Lin's short stories feature
in The Wales Collection
from Tim Saunders Publications
available in all good bookshops and online.

tsaunderspubs.weebly.com

TIM SAUNDERS PUBLICATIONS
publishes poetry, fiction and memoir

"Everybody has a book in them," according to
journalist Christopher Hitchens (1949 to 2011)

Do you have a book you would like to publish?

Email. tsaunderspubs@gmail.com

For more information visit:
tsaunderspubs.weebly.com

We are always on the look out for
poetry and short stories.

Printed in Great Britain
by Amazon